"Having trouble getting to sleep?"

Benedict's voice drifted softly out of the semidarkness.

She nearly jumped right off the bed. She had thought he was so soundly asleep that nothing would wake him.

"You should have warned me that you suffered from insomnia," he went on. "I might not have been so insistent on sharing a room with you!"

"I don't suffer from insomnia," Amy insisted indignantly. "I just have problems sleeping in a strange bed." And with a strange man only a few feet away, she nearly added.

To her utter relief, Benedict didn't say anything more. His breathing became very quiet again, but she wasn't fooled this time. He was no more asleep than she was.

JOANNA MANSELL finds writing hard work but very addictive. When she's not bashing away at her typewriter, she's usually got her nose buried in a book. She also loves gardening and daydreaming, two pastimes that go together remarkably well. The ambition of this Essex-born author is to write books that people will enjoy reading.

Books by Joanna Mansell

HARLEQUIN PRESENTS
1250—NIGHT WITH A STRANGER
1291—THE SEDUCTION OF SARA
1331—A KISS BY CANDLELIGHT
1364—DEVIL IN PARADISE
1394—EGYPTIAN NIGHTS
1436—HAUNTED SUMMER
1482—PAST SECRETS
1523—LAND OF DRAGONS

HARLEQUIN ROMANCE
2836—THE NIGHT IS DARK
2866—SLEEPING TIGER
2894—BLACK DIAMOND

JOANNA MANSELL

Istanbul Affair

Harlequin Books

TORONTO • NEW YORK • LONDON
AMSTERDAM • PARIS • SYDNEY • HAMBURG
STOCKHOLM • ATHENS • TOKYO • MILAN
MADRID • WARSAW • BUDAPEST • AUCKLAND

ISBN 0-373-11662-4

ISTANBUL AFFAIR

Copyright © 1991 by Joanna Mansell.

This edition published by arrangement with Harlequin Enterprises B. V.

® and ™ are trademarks of the publisher. Trademarks indicated with ® are registered in the United States Patent and Trademark Office, the Canadian Trade Marks Office and other countries.

Printed in U.S.A.

CHAPTER ONE

AMY ran her fingers distractedly through the silver-gold strands of her hair, and read the letter from her cousin, Angeline, for the dozenth time.

> Dear Amy, I'm in terrible trouble and danger. You must come to Istanbul at *once*. Book into the Golden Horn Hotel, and wait for someone to get in touch with you. Please, please don't let me down, or I don't know what will happen to me. And don't tell the police, or you might not see me again.

Angeline had scrawled her name at the bottom, her signature almost unrecognisable. In fact, the entire letter was barely legible. It was as if the writer had written it in tremendous haste—or her hand had been shaking so much that she could hardly hold the pen.

'This is crazy,' Amy muttered to herself. 'No one would want to hurt Angeline. The letter's got to be some sort of practical joke.'

A loud knocking on the door made her jump violently, and she realised how much the letter had set her nerves on edge. A glance at her watch told her that she was late in opening the shop. She was in no state to deal with a customer, though. Whoever it was would just have to come back later.

She was just reading the letter through yet again when there was another impatient knock on the door. Amy's green eyes flared. She got up, walked over to the door, yanked back the hefty bolts and whipped it open. Then she glared at the man standing outside.

'The shop is closed! It says so very clearly on the sign. Or can't you read?' she demanded, not caring in the least that she was being very rude.

The man glared straight back at her. 'I haven't come to buy any of this rubbish. I've come to talk to you. That is, if you're Amy Stewart.'

Amy's eyes took on an even fiercer glow. The antiques and curios that she sold might not be to everyone's taste, but they most certainly weren't rubbish!

'I'm Amy Stewart,' she informed him, her voice laced with intense dislike. 'But I can't see anyone right now. You'll have to come back at some other time.'

She began to slam the door shut, but he neatly inserted one foot in it. Then, with one easy movement of his arm, he pushed the door open again and strode right into the small, cluttered shop.

'If you don't get out of here in five seconds——' she threatened him.

'You'll do what?' he said coolly. 'Throw me out?'

He was standing very close to her now, towering over her, letting her see just how tall and powerful he was. Amy suddenly felt small, helpless and vulnerable, and she didn't like it, not one little bit.

She moved quickly to the back of the shop and reached under the counter.

'There's a burglar alarm here, and it's connected directly to the police station,' she told him tautly. 'If you don't leave immediately, I'll press it. The police will be here in just minutes.'

'Oh, this is ridiculous!' the man said with a quick wave of impatience. 'I haven't come here to rob or rape you. I simply want to talk to you about your cousin, Angeline.'

Amy blinked at him. 'Angeline?' she repeated. 'You know my cousin?'

He looked back at her steadily. 'Yes, I know Angeline.'

'And do you know where she is?'

'Of course. She's in Istanbul, on holiday. I haven't heard a word from her since she left, though. No phone-calls, no letters, not even a postcard. That's why I've called round to see you; I want to know if you've heard anything from her.'

'How did you know about me and where to find me?'

'Angeline's talked about you several times,' said the man. 'And when we drove past here once, she pointed out this shop and said that this was where you lived and worked.' His gaze became impatient again. 'Well?' he demanded. '*Has* she been in touch with you?'

Amy slid her hand into the pocket of her jeans. She had shoved Angeline's letter in there when she had first gone to the door. She didn't immediately pull it out and show it to this man, though. After all, she didn't know who he was. She didn't even know his name. She certainly wasn't going to confide in a perfect stranger.

'Angeline didn't tell me that she was going on holiday to Istanbul,' she said rather evasively.

'I shouldn't think that she told you everything that was going on in her life,' he replied brusquely. 'I got the impression that the two of you weren't particularly close.'

'Then why should she get in touch with me?' Amy parried.

His eyes suddenly narrowed. They were very dark eyes, she noticed irrelevantly. Almost as dark as his hair. And they seemed to see far too much.

'You know something, don't you?' he said with absolute certainty. 'Has she written? Phoned? What did she say?'

For a moment, Amy very nearly blurted out everything. It would be a huge relief to share it with someone—all the puzzlement and alarm that had bubbled through her as she had read Angeline's letter. Then her mouth set in a more stubborn line. She didn't want to share *anything* with this man. Anyhow, it was fairly obvious that he couldn't help in any way. If he could, Angeline would have written that frantic letter to him, instead of to her.

'I haven't heard from Angeline for ages,' she lied. 'If she hasn't been in touch with you, then she's probably got a very good reason. In fact, she's——'

Amy had been about to say that Angeline had probably met someone else and immediately lost all interest in this man now standing in front of her. Just in time, she stopped herself. He would soon find out for himself that Angeline had a very short attention-span when it came to men. 'After a few weeks, you know absolutely everything about them,' Angeline had said carelessly, more than once. 'All about their job, their family, their background, their boring likes and dislikes—and what they're like in bed. Then it's time to move on to the next one.'

Amy didn't approve or disapprove of her cousin's way of life. It was just the way that Angeline was. And if she was in the process of dumping this man for someone else, then Amy didn't want to get involved. Of course, it didn't explain that strange and worrying letter from her cousin, but, since this man obviously wasn't involved in the mystery, he couldn't help to solve it. What she had to do now was to get rid of him, so she could read that letter through yet again, and try to figure out exactly what was going on—and what she should do about it.

'Look,' she said in a very reasonable tone of voice, 'there's probably a perfectly simple explanation why she hasn't contacted you. Perhaps there's been trouble with the phone lines from Istanbul. Why don't you just go home and wait to hear from her? There's every chance that Angeline will ring you in the next couple of days.'

The man's dark gaze rested on her levelly, as if assessing everything she had said to him. Amy's heart began to sink. If he knew that she had lied to him, then she would *never* get rid of him.

A few moments later, though, he gave a brief nod of his head. 'You're probably right. Something's stopped her from getting in touch.' His eyes flicked over her. 'Are you sure you can't tell me what it is?'

'No, of course not,' Amy said quickly. 'She'll probably explain everything when she does finally get through to you.'

That distinctly disturbing gaze of his ran over her yet again, and this time it seemed to leave a small trail of shivers in its wake. Then he wheeled round and strode out of the shop, to Amy's intense relief.

She discovered that she had actually been holding her breath. She released it in a loud, shaky sigh as he disappeared from sight. Then she hurried through to the small room at the back of the shop, and pulled Angeline's letter out of her pocket.

As she skimmed through it, her eyebrows drew together in an anxious frown. What kind of trouble and danger could Angeline possibly be in? And why hadn't she told Amy more about it, so that she knew exactly what to do to help?

She stared at her cousin's scrawled writing with worried bewilderment. Then she gave a slightly exasperated sigh. Reading and re-reading the letter wasn't going to help. She already knew it by heart, and there weren't any subtle clues in it that she had missed.

Just then, a hand reached over her shoulder and ripped the sheet of paper away from her. Amy spun round, and found herself facing the man who had forcefully pushed his way into her shop just a short time ago.

He must have moved as silently as a big cat. She hadn't heard any footsteps or a whisper of movement. It was alarming to think that a large, powerful man could move so silently.

'I knew that you were lying,' he said tersely, as his dark gaze skimmed over the letter. 'I just didn't know why. I still don't know.'

'Because this is nothing to do with you,' Amy hissed back at him, her heart thundering away at a very unhealthy rate. 'That letter was written to *me*. Angeline doesn't mention you, or ask me to get in touch with you. If Angeline's got some kind of problem, then I'll deal with it without any help from you.'

'*If* Angeline's got some kind of problem?' he repeated incredulously. 'This letter was clearly written under duress, and she was obviously terrified when she wrote it. Just how much of problem does she have to have before you react in a normal, human manner?'

Amy's green eyes flashed angrily. 'I'm certainly worried about my cousin. But you don't know her——'

'I think that I know her a damned sight better than you seem to,' he interrupted, his own features darkening.

But Amy very much doubted that. Men only ever saw one side of Angeline. They didn't know about the little tricks she liked to play—some of them simply annoying, many of them downright malicious. They didn't know that her life was spent in the restless pursuit of the next thrill, the next piece of excitement.

Then Amy sighed. Despite everything, there were times when she realised that she was still rather fond of her cousin. And she thought that Angeline returned that affection in a careless, unthinking way. She supposed that was why Angeline had written to her, now that she was obviously in deep trouble.

'All right,' she said at last, reluctantly, 'the letter's probably genuine. It would have been more helpful, though, if Angeline had told me what *kind* of trouble she was in.'

'Perhaps she wasn't given the chance. Maybe this was all she was allowed to write. When are you leaving for Istanbul?'

'When—or even if—I'm going is absolutely none of your business,' she shot back, with a fresh spurt of annoyance.

'Oh, you're going,' he informed her, in a grim tone. 'Even if I have to drag you out there personally.'

'I've a business to run,' she reminded him in a very cold voice. 'I can't run off to the other side of the world at a moment's notice.'

'This shop full of rubbish is more important than your cousin's safety?' His mouth set in a line of pure contempt. 'Angeline was right. You really do dislike her, don't you?'

At that, Amy's anger vanished and her mouth dropped open slightly. 'Angeline thinks that I dislike her?'

'I don't know why you should,' he went on, his features still very clearly registering his own feelings on the subject. 'After all, you're the one with all the advantages, aren't you? Parents who are still alive, a stable home background, your own business—and, of course, all that money from your uncle. Most people would have been pretty bitter and resentful about that. Angeline wasn't, though. She just shrugged it off, said that if her uncle wanted to cut her out of his will, then that was OK by her. She earned good money as a model, she could make her own way in life. I admired her for taking that attitude.'

Amy had gone quite stiff while he was talking. Angeline had had no business telling all those very personal details to a stranger. Except he probably wasn't a stranger to Angeline by now, she reminded herself with a suddenly resigned shrug. Her cousin soon got to know the men in her life very intimately!

'Angeline didn't exactly have a deprived childhood,' she told him crisply. 'Her parents didn't die until she was nearly twenty. She had lived away from home for three years by then, and she hardly ever went back to see them. I got the impression that she didn't actually miss them very much. She's very self-sufficient.'

'That isn't the way that Angeline tells it. She said that her world fell apart when her parents died. She missed them all the time, that she hasn't really got over their deaths, even now.' His gaze slid over her coldly. 'Perhaps you don't actually know your cousin very well.'

Amy had always thought that she had understood Angeline only too well. She was beginning to feel just a little confused, though. This man seemed so certain about everything he was telling her. And although there were a great many things about him that she definitely didn't like or admire, he didn't seem the type who could be easily fooled by anyone. In fact, he appeared to be able to see the truth only too clearly. He had known at once that she was lying when she had told him she hadn't heard from Angeline. Surely he would have known just as easily if Angeline had lied to him?

What if she had been very wrong about her cousin? Amy thought with growing unease. What if all that glitz and glitter had just been a façade, hiding some very deep feelings and emotions that Angeline hadn't wanted the world to see? Perhaps he was right, and she hadn't really known her cousin at all. That was a highly disturbing notion, and one that she needed time to think about.

He didn't intend to give her any time for anything, however. 'When are you leaving for Istanbul?' he enquired curtly, for the second time.

'I—I don't know.' She was feeling distinctly confused and flustered now, and she didn't like it. He was hustling her along far too fast. 'There are phonecalls I'll have to make. I can't just leave at a moment's notice——'

He had almost forced her into admitting that she was actually going to Istanbul. A few minutes ago, she had been a long way away from making any such decision. Now he practically had her booked on the plane!

He glanced at his watch. 'I'll give you a couple of hours,' he told her. 'I'll be back at twelve, to find out what arrangements you've made.'

Amy glared at him with intense dislike. 'There's no need for you to come back at all!'

He gave her a thin and totally humourless smile. 'I wouldn't want to deprive you of the pleasure of seeing me again.'

She continued to glare at him. He obviously knew just how much she disliked him. It was equally obvious that he didn't care. He simply wanted to force her to abandon everything at a moment's notice and go careering off to Istanbul in search of Angeline.

'Twelve o'clock,' he repeated. 'And by the way, in case you're interested—my name is Benedict Kane.'

Amy wanted to yell that she wasn't interested in one single thing about him, but it was already too late. He had moved quickly and silently out of the shop, disappearing as swiftly as he had come.

After he had gone, she ran and bolted the door to the shop. She didn't want anyone else coming in this morning. Any prospective customers would just have to wait until she felt ready to face the world again. And after Angeline's letter and that visit from Benedict Kane, that could take some time!

She prowled back to the room behind the shop, slumped into a chair and stared at the wall. When she had woken up this morning she had thought this was going to be just another Monday. It was traditionally a quiet day, with few customers. She usually spent the morning dusting and tidying up the shop, had a leisurely lunch, and then caught up with any paperwork in the afternoon.

Instead, she was sitting here wondering how long she was going to have to stay in Istanbul, and what she was going to find when she got there.

Amy realised, with a rather depressed sigh, that she had finally accepted that she would have to go. There had been something very disturbing about that letter from Angeline—a slightly hysterical tone to it that her sophisticated cousin wouldn't have used under normal circumstances.

She stayed slumped in the chair for some time, trying to figure out what could have happened to Angeline. She even read the letter through again, although that didn't help in the least. In the end, she gave another sigh, hauled herself out of the chair, and went to phone her mother.

'Hello, Mum,' she said, as the receiver was picked up at the other end. 'I want to ask you a favour. Can you look after the shop for a day or two? Perhaps even longer?'

'I'd love to,' her mother said at once.

Amy gave a small, wry smile. Her mother adored looking after the shop on the odd occasions when she had to go out, or was away on a buying trip. The only trouble was, she was absolutely hopeless at it! She would cheerfully knock ten or even twenty pounds off an item if she thought a customer looked a little short of money, the till-receipts never balanced at the end of the day, and because she thought everyone was as honest as she was, she never noticed if a small ornament disappeared into the pocket of a shoplifter.

On one memorable occasion, a thief had calmly walked out with a three-foot-high brass elephant. Her mother had even opened the door for him!

'I thought he had paid for it earlier and had come back to collect it,' she had explained disarmingly.

'If you thought that, you should have asked to see the receipt,' Amy had groaned.

'I didn't like to,' her mother replied comfortably. 'He seemed such a nice gentleman. If I'd asked to see the receipt, it would have looked as if I didn't trust him.'

'But he was a thief!' Amy had said a little despairingly. 'You'd have been right not to have trusted him.'

'Oh well, it was only an elephant,' said her mother philosophically. 'I expect you'll soon be able to get your hands on another one.'

The loss of the elephant had effectively wiped out Amy's profits for that week, and she had sworn she would never ask her mother to look after the shop again. Yet here she was, back on the phone to her, asking her to look after it not just for an afternoon, but for a few days! Businesswise, this was definitely suicidal! There just wasn't anyone else she could ask, though. Her father and all of her friends worked full-time. She would just have to hope that her mother didn't do anything too disastrous while she was away.

'Where are you going?' asked her mother. 'You're not due to go off on another buying trip just yet, are you?'

'I'm going to Istanbul.'

'Isn't that rather extravagant?' said her mother doubtfully. 'I mean, I expect you'll be able to find some fascinating curios in the bazaars, but you won't make very much profit after you've paid your air fare and hotel bill.'

'I'm not going on a buying trip. In fact I don't want to go at all. I've had this very odd letter from Angeline, though. It looks as if she's got herself into some serious trouble, and she wants me to go and bail her out.'

'Angeline's always in trouble,' said her mother disapprovingly. 'And most of it's of her own making. I think you should ignore her letter, Amy. If she's in a mess, then let her get herself out of it. I don't want her dragging you into some risky situation. Anyway, what's she doing in Istanbul?'

'She went there on holiday, and no one's heard from her since she left. I don't think I've got much choice except to go out there for a couple of days, and try to find out what's going on.'

'And do you think Angeline would drop everything and go rushing halfway round the world if *you* were in trouble?' said her mother tartly.

Amy knew that her mother didn't particularly like Angeline, even though she was her niece. Perhaps that was part of the problem, she thought with a small sigh. No one in their family had liked Angeline very much. On the other hand, Angeline had never gone out of her way to make herself liked. Quite the opposite, in fact. Amy had long suspected that her cousin rather enjoyed being the black sheep of the family.

'Look, Mum,' she said rather tiredly, 'I've made up my mind about this. I'm going to Istanbul. I just want to know if you'll look after the shop while I'm away. If you won't, I'll just shut it down for a few days.'

'I've already said that I will,' replied her mother promptly. 'Anyway, you can't shut it down. You'll lose customers.'

'I can afford to run it at a loss for a while if I have to.'

'And you can easily afford the fare to Istanbul, thanks to that money your uncle left you. Does that have something to do with the reason you're rushing off to try and help Angeline?' asked her mother shrewdly. 'You're still feeling guilty because you got all the money, and Angeline didn't get a penny?'

'It doesn't seem at all fair,' admitted Amy. 'And it does make me feel—well, as if I owe her something.'

'Does she know that you wanted to give her half? But that the terms of your uncle's will didn't allow it?'

'No,' said Amy. 'There didn't seem much point in telling her, since there's no way to break the terms of his will.'

Her uncle had left her the money on the proviso that she didn't touch any of the capital for five years, unless it was for business purposes. She had used some of it to pay for the lease on her small shop, and to buy stock. That had only made a very small dent in it, though. Her uncle had left her a sizeable legacy, thanks to some very shrewd investments. And although she wasn't allowed to touch the capital, she was allowed to keep and spend the annual interest on the investments. That meant she could easily pay for her ticket to Istanbul, hotel bills and any extra expenses.

'You're absolutely determined to go?' said her mother with some resignation.

'Yes,' Amy said firmly. Any lingering doubts had finally vanished. If she just ignored Angeline's letter, she wouldn't be able to sleep at nights for worrying about her wayward cousin. 'Can you come round tomorrow morning? If I've already left, I'll leave the keys to the shop with Mrs Baker next door.'

'Just be careful,' warned her mother. 'Don't let Angeline drag you into anything stupid or dangerous.'

'I won't,' promised Amy, and it was a promise that she definitely intended to keep. If Angeline needed practical help, then she would give it, if she could. But if her problem involved a man—or men!—then Angeline was on her own. Amy didn't feel inclined, or qualified, to give advice or help on that subject.

After her mother had rung off, Amy wandered a little restlessly round her small flat over the shop. What should she pack? How long would she be away? Should she try and book a hotel-room before she left, or wait until she got there?

Unable to make even simple decisions, she went back down to the shop. This was ridiculous! she told herself with some impatience. If she was going to leave in the morning, then she needed to get organised right now.

The trouble was, of course, that she didn't actually want to go. She liked her life the way it was at the moment, quiet and uncomplicated, with only the running of the shop to think about. It was a period of calm after a long season of storms. And she wanted it to stay that way. She wasn't ready yet for problems and emotional turmoil, and that was what she was likely to get caught up in if she got involved in her cousin's life.

The door to the shop rattled and, without thinking, Amy went to open it. She had half drawn back the bolt when she suddenly glanced at her watch. Twelve o'clock! That meant that it was almost certainly Benedict Kane on the other side of the door.

For a few moments, she seriously considered keeping him locked out. Then she gave a resigned sigh. She had the feeling that Mr Kane wouldn't let a small thing like a bolted door stand in his way. The best thing would be to let him in, and tell him that she was going to do whatever she could to help Angeline. That should finally satisfy him. She could then get rid of him and, with any luck, never set eyes on him again.

Amy drew the bolt back fully. An instant later, Benedict Kane pushed the door wide open and strode back into the shop.

'Didn't anyone ever teach you that it's basic good manners to wait to be invited in?' Amy enquired, scowling at him angrily.

'I haven't the time to be polite,' he replied shortly. 'There's too much to be done. Have you made any arrangements yet for going to Istanbul?'

She continued to scowl at him. There was something about this man that set every one of her nerves right on edge. A few moments ago, she had been almost ready to co-operate with him. Now that she was face to face with him again, though, she had already changed her mind about that. She suddenly decided that she wanted him out of her shop, and out of her life. Let Angeline deal with him when she finally got back to England. Benedict Kane was her cousin's problem, not hers!

'I haven't made any travel arrangements yet, but I will be going to Istanbul, and I will help Angeline if I possibly can,' she said in a very stiff voice. 'And as far as I'm concerned, that's all you need to know. I'd appreciate it if you'd leave now. This is a family matter, and you're not family, Mr Kane. In fact, as far as I can see, you're just someone that Angeline's known for a very short time. I think that you've interfered in our lives quite enough.'

He didn't budge an inch. She hadn't really thought that he would. This wasn't a man who was used to taking orders from anyone.

'I see that there are one or two things that you still don't understand,' he said softly.

Amy discovered that she didn't like that low tone of voice. There was something far more disturbing about it than a voice raised in plain anger.

'I think that I understand everything perfectly,' she returned. 'You're pushing yourself in where you're not wanted. I don't want to be rude, but where you're concerned it's very hard to be anything else! So I'll tell you just one more time, and I'll make it absolutely plain, so that you finally get the message. I want you to stop interfering and I want you to leave.'

His dark eyes became almost black as they fixed on her face. 'Now let *me* make something clear,' he said, in a tone that sent a whole cascade of goose-pimples down her spine. 'I'm not going anywhere until Angeline's back in England, safe and well. I don't trust you to make much of an effort to get her out of whatever trouble she's in. As far as I can see, you've got very little feeling for your cousin. You probably wouldn't care too much if you never set eyes on her again.'

'How dare you say that?' Amy howled in pure outrage. 'Angeline and I might not be very close, but I'd certainly never abandon her if she were in serious trouble. Anyway, I've already said that I'll go to Istanbul.'

'I know that you'll go,' Benedict Kane agreed grimly. 'In fact, I've already booked your ticket for you.'

'You've what?' she said furiously.

'Booked your ticket,' he repeated, his dark eyes still fixed intently on her face.

'I don't need you to make my travel arrangements for me!'

'I just want to make sure you get there.'

'And how are you going to do that?' she enquired heatedly. 'Put me on the plane personally?'

'Something like that,' he said, sounding much more unperturbed now. 'Except that I won't just be putting you on the plane. I'll be getting on it with you.'

'You'll *what*?' Amy yelped.

'I'm coming with you to Istanbul.'

'Oh, no, you're not!' she shot back at once.

'The arrangements are already made.'

'Then you can just unmake them. I'm not going *anywhere* with you!'

A dangerous light began to flicker in his eyes. 'Don't you think that, just for once, you could stop thinking about what *you* want. Try thinking of Angeline for just a couple of minutes,' he advised tersely. 'Or are you so self-centered that that just isn't possible?'

'I don't see how it will possibly help Angeline to have you trailing all the way out to Istanbul,' Amy said promptly. 'I've already told you, she wrote that letter to *me*. She didn't ask me to get in touch with you, and she certainly didn't tell me to ask you for help. I know that you've said the two of you are close, but I'm beginning to wonder if you're telling the truth about that. After all, in that letter she didn't even mention your name.'

'Perhaps she wasn't allowed to mention it.'

Amy stared at him. 'Just what do you mean by that?'

'Perhaps she didn't write that letter of her own accord. Maybe someone forced her to write it—and told her what to put in it.'

Her green gaze became wary. 'What are you saying?'

Benedict Kane looked directly back at her. 'I think there's a strong possibility that Angeline's been kidnapped.'

'But—that's ridiculous!' Disbelief echoed clearly in her voice. 'Who on earth would want to kidnap Angeline? And why? Anyway, what would they get out of it? She doesn't have any close family who'd pay a ransom to get her back. And although she earns good money as a model, she spends just about every penny she makes. She doesn't have any money of her own that she could give them in exchange for her release.'

'That's right,' he agreed. 'But she does have a cousin who looks very much like her. The same pale blonde hair, tall, slim body, fair skin and beautiful face. And this cousin *does* have money—a large sum of it, inherited from an uncle. What if they snatched the wrong girl?' he suggested softly. 'Took Angeline instead of *you*?'

Amy swallowed very hard. 'Instead of me?' she managed to get out at last in a very squeaky little voice.

Benedict Kane shrugged. 'It's just a theory. But right now it's the only one that seems to make any sense. Perhaps someone found out about that money you inherited from your uncle—and decided this was an easy way of getting his hands on it.'

'But the money's all tied up in trust. I can't touch a penny of the capital. I'm only allowed to spend the interest.'

'The trust could probably be untied—especially if it meant saving your life.'

'But—kidnapping? Who on earth would do such a thing?' Amy said shakily.

'Someone fairly ruthless and amoral. Perhaps someone who learned about the money quite by chance—through the friend of a friend, or perhaps through some business connection.'

'I don't think I believe any of this,' she said in a defensive tone. 'None of it adds up. I mean, if they did grab Angeline instead of me, why do it in Istanbul? Why not here, in England?'

'I don't know. I can't answer any of your questions, I can only tell you what I think might have happened.'

'But I don't really look like Angeline,' she said a little desperately. 'She's taller, thinner, prettier, more— oh, just more of everything!'

Benedict Kane looked at her with some surprise. 'You don't look the type to have an inferiority complex.'

'I don't,' she denied at once. 'That's just the way that Angeline sometimes makes me feel.'

'But you will try and help her?'

'I've already said that I will. But if she *has* been kidnapped, then the obvious thing is to go to the police.'

'She warned you in her letter not to do that,' he reminded her.

'But I can't handle something like that by myself!'

'That's why I'm coming with you.'

'I don't *want* you to come with me,' she shouted at him, her frayed nerves suddenly giving way.

His dark gaze stared straight into her over-bright green eyes.

'I'm getting very tired of hearing what you want and don't want. And there isn't time for any more pointless arguments. A delay of even a day might be disastrous for Angeline. In the morning, we're leaving for Istanbul—both of us—so be ready when I come round to pick you up. And remember this. If you cause me any trouble, or do anything that puts Angeline's life in danger, then you most certainly won't like the consequences!'

Amy wanted to say something, but couldn't. Something in Benedict Kane's eyes and the tone of his voice had made her throat go totally dry.

This man is dangerous, warned a small voice inside her head. But she already knew that. She had known it from the moment when he had first walked into her shop.

And now he was going to Istanbul with her, and she couldn't see any way of stopping him. Amy didn't like that. She didn't like it at all.

She also had the feeling that she definitely *wasn't* going to enjoy the next few days.

CHAPTER TWO

RIGHT up until the moment when she boarded the plane for Istanbul, Amy tried to think of some way of getting away from Benedict Kane. As he settled himself into the seat beside her, she finally had to admit defeat. She was stuck with him, at least for the next few hours. Once they reached Istanbul, though, she was determined that things were going to change. He wanted to find Angeline? Fine, he could go and look for her by himself!

Amy remembered his theory about Angeline being kidnapped—perhaps even being grabbed instead of *her*—but finally wrinkled her nose and discounted it. The whole thing was just too far-fetched. She was willing to bet that the trouble Angeline was in was a lot more personal—and probably involved a man.

She shot a quick sideways glance at Benedict Kane as he sat beside her. He looked very relaxed and yet alert, like a great cat that was almost, but not quite, asleep.

He had picked her up early that morning in his car, which was dark and streamlined, with an engine that purred with lightly restrained power. They hadn't spoken a word to each other during the drive to the airport, nor while they had waited to board the plane. He seemed totally uninterested in her as a person. Her only value to him was as Angeline's cousin, which meant that she might be able to help him to find her.

Amy glanced at him again. He was a lot less formally dressed than he had been yesterday, when he had worn a dark, well-cut suit. Today he had on jeans and a sweatshirt, but they fitted so perfectly that they might have been made for him. In fact, they probably *had* been made for him, Amy decided with a small scowl. The man reeked of money. He probably didn't know what it was like to buy something off-the-peg!

She didn't mean to look at him any more, but there was nothing to see out of the small window except low cloud, and she found her gaze wandering back to him. This time he looked straight back at her, his dark eyes studying her thoughtfully, as if he were seeing her properly for the first time that day.

'You don't like me, do you?' he said calmly at last.

Amy hadn't expected him to say anything like that. Slightly flustered, she dragged her eyes away from him and stared ahead instead.

'I don't have to like you, do I?'

'No, you don't,' he agreed. 'But it might make things rather difficult over the next few days if we can't manage at least to be polite to each other.'

'Well, there's one obvious solution,' Amy said promptly. 'Once we get to Istanbul, we can split up. We'll both look for Angeline, and whoever finds her first can contact the other, to let them know she's safe and well.'

'And what if she isn't safe and well?'

'I'm sure she will be,' Amy said firmly. 'Angeline knows how to look after herself.'

'Then you've convinced yourself that she isn't in any real danger? That she's got herself into some silly scrape, but nothing more serious?'

'I don't believe that she's been kidnapped, if that's what you mean,' Amy said with growing certainty.

'What about the letter she sent you?'

'That was just Angeline being over-dramatic. She's probably already sorry that she sent it, and hoping that I'm not rushing out intent on rescuing her. Which I am, thanks to you!' she finished, with another scowl. 'I still don't know how I let you push me into this. It's the craziest thing I've done for a long time.'

'You don't usually do things on impulse?'

'No, definitely not.' At least, not any more, she reminded herself with a small shiver.

'Then you're really not like Angeline, are you?' he said. There was the faintest hint of amusement in his voice, and for some reason that annoyed Amy.

'I've already told you that I'm not,' she snapped.

'Do you wish that you were?'

For a moment, Amy found herself actually considering his question. *Did* she want to be more like her cousin, whizzing in and out of different relationships, with no scars to mark their ending because there was never any serious involvement in the first place? She gave a brief sigh. It would certainly be more comfortable to be like that!

'The two of you *are* alike in some ways,' Benedict went on. 'But you obviously lead very different lives. Do you resent Angeline's successful career in modelling? Are you jealous of your cousin?'

That jolted Amy out of her introspective thoughts. 'Definitely not!' she said vehemently. 'Who needs glitzy looks, a hectic lifestyle and a whole stream of flashy men?'

At that, the amusement vanished from Benedict's eyes. In its place came an expression that was a lot less affable. Amy realised that her last remark had probably sounded completely bitchy. She didn't particularly care, though. It didn't matter if this man had a low opinion of her. Whatever he thought of her, it simply wasn't important.

A rather tense silence stretched between them which Amy eventually decided to break because she was finding it rather uncomfortable.

'How did you meet Angeline?' she asked, deciding to try to keep the conversation on more neutral ground. An aeroplane wasn't a very good place to have a stand-up row!

'One of my companies deals with the fashion trade and has its own mail-order catalogue,' he replied, after a short pause. 'Angeline was one of the models we hired when we began photographing the new season's catalogue.'

One of his companies? thought Amy, her eyebrows drawing together expressively. Just how many did the man own?

'When I first saw her, something just clicked,' Benedict went on. 'All of my adult life, I feel as if I've been looking for someone. Angeline's the closest I've come to finding that person.'

'You mean that you've been looking for someone special, and you think that it's Angeline?' Amy said a little incredulously. At the same time, she felt a totally unexpected pang of pity for him. If he thought that Angeline was the perfect partner he had been searching for, then she suspected he was in for a grave disappointment! Unless, of course, her cousin had changed dramatically over the past few weeks—and Amy didn't think that was very likely.

He obviously thought that he had said enough—perhaps more than enough—because he fell silent after that. Amy didn't make any effort to restart the conversation. The silence that fell between them wasn't uncomfortable this time, and she eventually closed her eyes and tried to pretend that he wasn't even there.

The plane droned on and, after a while, she dozed. When she finally woke up again, it was a few moments before she could remember where she was. Then she turned her head, saw Benedict Kane's distinctive features, and gave a silent groan. She was on her way to Istanbul on a wild-goose chase!

She realised that she had woken up because Benedict had touched her arm. She could still feel the warmth of his fingers resting against her skin. As if realising that she didn't like the unexpected contact between them, he smoothly drew his hand away. Then he nodded towards the seatbelt sign, which was lit.

'We'll be landing in a few minutes.'

At any other time she would have thoroughly enjoyed this trip and been looking forward to her first sight of Istanbul. Right now, though, she felt tired, despite her long nap, and distinctly irritable.

By the time she finally plodded off the plane, she was wondering what on earth she was doing here. It was late afternoon by now, and it already felt like a very long day!

The sun was beating down out of a clear blue sky, and she put on dark glasses, to cut out the glare.

'It's several miles to the centre of the city. We'll have to take a taxi,' instructed Benedict.

'Yes, O Master,' she murmured sarcastically under her breath, and trudged after him as he headed purposefully towards the nearest taxi.

Once they were settled inside, however, and rattling off towards the city, Amy took off her dark glasses and turned to him with new determination.

'I think that it's time we got a few things straight. I don't mind sharing this taxi with you, but once we reach the city I intend that we should split up. You can find your own hotel and start your own search for Angeline. In fact, it'll be much better if we do things that way,' she went on firmly. 'We can cover twice as much ground if we're working individually.'

Benedict didn't even answer. That really annoyed her, and she glared at him.

'Did you hear what I just said?' she demanded loudly.

'Of course,' he said calmly. 'It would be rather hard not to, when you're yelling right in my ear. But there's no question of us splitting up. I've already booked both of us into the Golden Horn hotel.'

'You had no right to do that!'

'It was the obvious thing to do,' he replied, his voice still irritatingly unruffled. 'I was simply following the instructions in Angeline's letter. She told us to book into the Golden Horn hotel, and that's what I've done.'

'She told *me* to book into that hotel,' Amy said furiously. 'That letter didn't even mention you!'

'Then she'll have a surprise when she finds I've turned up.'

'Well, I hope it's a *pleasant* surprise,' Amy said meaningfully.

'I think Angeline will be pleased to see me,' he said with an arrogant confidence that really grated on her nerves.

Not if Angeline's already found a replacement for you, Amy muttered under her breath. She was careful not to let him hear what she had said, though. She wasn't stupid. And she definitely didn't intend to be around when he met up with Angeline again. She had the feeling that that could turn out to be a very explosive encounter!

In the meantime, she had to cope with the problem of his staying at the same hotel. Gloomily, she contemplated the prospect. It meant that they would be bumping into each other at meal times. On top of that, he would be watching out for her whenever she left the hotel, and probably even wanting to come with her, in case she led him to Angeline.

No! Amy decided, with a small shudder. That was *not* what she wanted. And that meant she had to put a stop to it right now.

'I'm going to stay at the Golden Horn hotel,' she told him. 'But I want you to find somewhere else to stay.' When he didn't answer, her green eyes began to darken. 'Why are you ignoring me?' she demanded.

'I'm simply trying to avoid yet another argument,' he replied, in an unexpectedly weary voice. 'I've made certain arrangements, and I don't intend to alter them in any way, so there doesn't seem much point in discussing the matter any further.'

But Amy had had just about enough of this. 'You've barged into my life, interfered in my personal affairs, and made arrangements that concern me without even consulting me. Well, this is where it stops! I can't stop you from staying in Istanbul and looking for Angeline, but I *don't* have to have you hanging round my neck like some bloody great albatross all the time! If you won't move out of the

Golden Horn hotel, then I will. I'll find somewhere to stay that's quiet, private, and a long way away from you!'

His own eyes had taken on an ominous expression, and Amy gave a small, involuntary inner shiver. She had forgotten that this man could be very intimidating when he put his mind to it.

Benedict twisted round so that he was facing her, and his hands suddenly shot out and gripped her shoulders very hard. Amy winced as his fingers dug into her skin, but refused to look scared or daunted. He *wasn't* going to browbeat her with sheer physical force.

He shook her fairly fiercely. Then, still without letting go of her, he loomed nearer so that his dark gaze blazed only inches away from her own.

'I've had enough of listening to your self-centred babbling,' he said through gritted teeth. 'You obviously don't give a damn about your cousin or what happens to her, but I do. No matter what's happened to her or what sort of trouble or danger she's in, I intend to get her safely back again. Unfortunately, I need your help to do that. But I'm going to make sure that I get that help! I don't much care what I have to do to ensure that you co-operate with me every step of the way, but believe this. You *will* help me. The only choice you have is whether you do it voluntarily or have to be forced into it. Doing it voluntarily will make it much pleasanter and easier for both of us, but if I have to do it by any other means, then I will. Do you understand me?'

Amy swallowed very hard. She understood only too clearly! And she realised that she had seriously underestimated this man. She had thought that he was dangerous. Now she knew that he was much more than that.

'Yes, I understand,' she muttered at last. And, hard though she tried, she couldn't quite keep a betraying tremor out of her voice.

But he didn't release her. Instead, his grip on her shoulders tightened.

'And you believe that I'll do whatever I have to do to get results?'

Oh, yes, she believed him! This time, she couldn't quite get the words out, though. Her throat seemed to have dried up completely. Instead, she gave a jerky nod.

Yet still he didn't let go of her. 'Tell me which hotel you're going to book into,' he instructed softly.

'The G—G——' Her voice croaked drily as she tried to stammer out the words.

'I can't quite hear you,' he prompted relentlessly.

Oh, she hated this man! she told herself with frustrated fury. No one had *ever* treated her like this before.

'The Golden Horn hotel,' she managed to get out at last, almost spitting the words at him.

At long last, he released the hard grip of his fingers. Amy rubbed her bruised shoulders and glared at him resentfully. 'If you behave like this with Angeline, then I think you're going to have a very short-lived relationship!'

A strange smile touched the corners of his mouth. 'I behave very differently when I'm with Angeline. But then, she's a very different kind of girl.'

'She certainly is!' Amy muttered. Perhaps her only consolation in all of this was that Benedict Kane was almost certainly in for a few shocks when he got to know Angeline rather better.

She stared out of the taxi window. They were rattling through the suburbs of Istanbul now. The streets were narrow, noisy, and packed with people, with the crowds thickening as they drew nearer to the centre of the city. Shops, offices and hotels were crammed close together, and there hardly seemed enough room for the congested streams of traffic trying to force their way through the maze of streets. They seemed to be getting caught up in one giant traffic jam which looked as if it would take the rest of the day and half the night to clear.

'Can't we go some other way?' Amy said irritably.

'If you're travelling by car, then you have to stick to the main roads. The side-roads are generally too steep or too narrow to take traffic. Unfortunately, we've hit the rush-hour. If we'd arrived an hour earlier or an hour later, the roads would still have been congested, but not nearly as bad as this.'

'It would be quicker to walk!'

'I doubt it,' he said drily.

Amy had to admit that he was probably right. The pavements were so thronged with people that trying to push through them, especially if you were loaded down with luggage, would be a very slow and frustrating business.

'How much longer before we reach the hotel?' she grumbled. Her temper still felt extremely frayed, and after everything that had happened she wasn't in the mood even to try to be pleasant to the man sitting beside her.

'We should be there fairly soon. It's in the old part of the city, near to a lot of the main tourist attractions. The Topkapi Palace, the Blue Mosque, the church of Haghia Sophia and the covered Bazaar are all close by.'

Amy looked at him with intense dislike. 'I didn't come to Istanbul because I wanted to go sightseeing.' She turned away from him again, pointedly ignoring him as she stared out of the window. Despite what she had said, though, she found her gaze drawn to the tall, slim minarets that shot skywards, and the occasional glimpses of the great domes of the mosques. And there was an exotic pungency in the air—although some people might simply call it a strong smell! she decided wryly. She found herself wishing that she could have come here under very different circumstances. She could have spent several happy days exploring the palaces and mosques, the narrow side-streets with their fascinating shops, and the bazaars, where just about everything under the sun was sold.

Instead, however, she was probably going to see little more than her hotel-room. She would be here just long enough to bail Angeline out of whatever trouble she was in; then she would have to shoot off back home before her mother sold the entire stock of her shop at such low prices that that it would take weeks for her profits to recover!

The taxi finally jolted to a halt outside a hotel that was situated down a road that seemed marginally quieter than the main thoroughfare they had just travelled along. Benedict paid the fare, and Amy realised for the first time that she didn't have any Turkish money. Worried about Angeline, and fretting about what would happen to the shop while she was away, there just hadn't been any spare time to think about or plan the trip to Istanbul. This morning, she had just slung some clothes into a bag, grabbed her passport, and left.

'Do you think the hotel will take credit cards?' she asked, as the taxi roared off in a cloud of exhaust fumes, leaving them standing outside the main entrance.

'I expect so,' said Benedict. 'But if you've a problem with money, why don't you let me pay for everything?' As her green eyes began to flash warningly, he added, 'I'm not offering to pay for your entire stay. I'm simply suggesting that we put everything on to one bill, and then you can pay me your share when this is all over. It would make things very much easier.'

'I'm not interested in making things easier,' Amy retorted. 'And I want to pay my own way from the very start.'

Benedict gave a resigned sigh. 'Then let me pay just for today. In the morning, you can go to the bank and change some money. You can pay all your own bills from then on.'

'All right,' she agreed grudgingly. She didn't like owing him anything for even one day, but she had to admit that his suggestion made sense.

He slung his bag over his shoulder, and went to pick up hers. Amy got there first, though.

'I can manage my own luggage,' she informed him stiffly.

His eyes went a shade darker. 'You're really going out of your way to make things difficult, aren't you?'

'No one's forcing you to stay,' she reminded him as she lugged her bag through into the hotel foyer. 'You can leave whenever you want.'

'I'm not going anywhere until I've found Angeline,' he said shortly, a grim expression settling across his face. 'And don't think you can get rid of me by continually being rude to me. It won't work. You've got to have a certain amount of feeling for someone to let them get to you. And I don't have any feelings about you at all.'

With that stinging remark, he walked over to the reception desk to book them in. Amy didn't follow him. Instead, she stood in one corner of the foyer feeling oddly shaken.

Of course, she didn't *care* that he had openly admitted to being completely indifferent towards her. She preferred it that way, she told herself with some determination. All the same, it wasn't very nice to hear someone say something like that to your face, even if it were Benedict Kane who had said it.

By the time he came back to her, she had got herself back under some kind of control. She arranged a stiff, cold expression on her face, and made no effort to smile even half-heartedly at him as he approached her.

'I've booked us in,' he said shortly, apparently as disinclined as she was to bother with even basic politeness. 'Let's go up.'

'Why did Angeline tell me to book into *this* hotel?' asked Amy with a frown, as they went towards the lift. 'Did she have a room here? Is she still here?'

Benedict briefly shook his head. 'I made enquiries at the reception desk. Angeline has never stayed here.'

As they got into the lift, Amy gave a frustrated sigh. 'None of this makes any sense. Why on earth couldn't Angeline have said more in her letter? She might at least have given me some clue as to what this is all about.'

'I've already told you what I think,' he reminded her, a rather grim note returning to his voice. 'I don't think she was allowed to say anything more in that letter.'

'Oh, your kidnapping theory,' she said dismissively. 'That's a non-starter, as far as I'm concerned.'

'Why?'

'Because things like that simply don't happen to people like us. And I don't buy that story about someone grabbing Angeline instead of me, either. We really don't look alike. It's very easy to tell us apart.'

The lift doors slid open and they walked out into the corridor.

'To someone who knows both of you, it's easy to tell you apart,' agreed Benedict. 'I'd certainly never mistake you for Angeline. Quite apart from the basic differences, like the colour of your eyes and the sound of your voice, you're quite different in character. Angeline's far more sweet-natured——'

At that, Amy couldn't suppress a great snort of laughter. 'Sweet-natured? *Angeline?*'

'I know that you like to run down your cousin at every opportunity,' said Benedict in a rather contemptuous tone. 'But for the next couple of days, you might as well hold your breath. I'm not interested in hearing all the unpleasant things you like to say about her.'

'Are *you* in for a surprise when you get to know Angeline rather better,' Amy murmured under her breath. She got the message, though. As far as Benedict Kane was concerned, Angeline could do no wrong. Heaven knew how her cousin had managed to keep up such an angelic image while she was with him, but she had certainly managed to fool him. Amy found she had a new respect for her cousin, because she was certain that there were very few people in this world who had managed to fool Mr Kane.

. He had come to a halt outside one of the doors now. He produced a key from his pocket, unlocked it, and walked inside.

Amy followed him in. 'Is this your room, or mine?' she asked. She hoped it was hers. She was tired and sweaty after the long journey. What she wanted right now was a hot shower and a change of clothes before dinner.

Benedict dumped his bag on the floor. 'It's our room,' he informed her calmly.

She stared at him warily. 'Just what do you mean by that?' she asked at last.

'I'd have thought it was self-explanatory.'

Unfortunately, it was. But she definitely didn't like the explanation!

'If you think for one moment that I'm sharing this room with you——' she began, her green eyes starting to glow very brightly.

'I hope that you're not going to be childish about this.'

'I don't think it's particularly childish not to want to sleep with someone you scarcely know and certainly don't like!' Amy retorted.

His dark eyebrow shot upwards. 'I'm certainly not asking you to sleep with me. I'm not interested in laying a single finger on you. But I do intend that we should share this room.'

'Well, I don't really care what you intend!' She picked up her bag and began to head towards the door. 'I'm going down to reception to book a separate room.'

He reached the door before her, moving so swiftly that all she saw was a blur of movement. With one sweep of his hand, he slammed it shut. Then he locked it and slid the key into his pocket.

For the first time, Amy began to feel afraid. Despite the amount of time they had spent together, she still knew very little about this man. She didn't know what he was capable of—what he might do, if he were thwarted over something.

'Look,' she said in a more placatory tone, hoping he couldn't hear just how very nervous she suddenly felt, 'perhaps we can talk this over.'

'That sounds like a sensible idea,' he agreed. His voice sounded relaxed, but his body was visibly tense, and there was a light in his eyes that she definitely didn't like.

'Er—could you unlock the door first? I think we could have a much more productive discussion if I didn't feel so—so——'

'Trapped?' he suggested softly.

That hadn't been the word she had been about to use. It made it sound as if he had the absolute upper hand, with all the advantages on his side.

'It makes me feel slightly claustrophobic, that's all,' she lied, hoping that those dark, clever eyes of his weren't seeing too far into her head and guessing the truth.

He took the key from his pocket and tossed it gently into the air a couple of times, playing with it—in the same way that he was playing with her.

'I'll open the door when this discussion is over,' he told her at last. 'I don't want you running out on me halfway through.'

'I won't do that. I promise.'

'But for all I know, your promises might be worth absolutely nothing.'

Amy opened her mouth, ready to argue vehemently with him, but then shut it again. This was getting her nowhere. It certainly wasn't getting her out of this room and away from Benedict Kane! The only way she was going to do that was by going along with this for now, and then making a dash for freedom at the very first opportunity that she got.

'All right,' she said, in what she hoped was a calm voice. 'What do you want to talk about?'

'The reason why I'm going to share this room with you.'

'We are *not*——' she began sharply. Then she stopped and made an effort to get her temper back under control. Shouting at him was going to achieve absolutely nothing. 'I'd have thought that you could understand perfectly well why I don't want to share a room with you,' she went on, in a much more reasonable tone of voice.

'Of course I understand,' he agreed calmly. But before she could breathe a sigh of relief, he added, 'But I still intend to stay here for the next day or two.'

'Why?' she demanded.

'Because I think that you'll soon be getting a phone-call concerning Angeline. And I want to be around when that call comes.'

Amy stared at him. 'You're still going along with that ridiculous idea of a kidnapping, aren't you? You think we're going to get some kind of ransom demand.'

'I think it's very likely,' he agreed.

She gave a heavy sigh. 'You're crazy. But I can't stop you believing all these wild ideas. I don't see why we have to share a room, though. Even if you're right—and I don't for one moment think you are—then I'll be here to answer the phone. I can tell you what they say.'

'You might decide not to tell me anything at all,' he pointed out.

Amy blinked. 'You think that I'd keep something like that from you? Is that why you're doing this? You don't trust me?'

'No, I don't,' Benedict replied in an unruffled voice, ignoring her growing indignation. 'As far as I can see, you've got a very odd relationship with your cousin. When she writes you a frantic letter asking for help, you don't take it at all seriously. In fact, if I hadn't been around, you might even have ignored it.'

'I wouldn't have done that!' she cut in angrily.

He took no notice. 'It looks as if you're going to have to be pushed into helping Angeline every step of the way. It also looks as if I'm the only one who cares enough to do that pushing.'

Amy gave him a fierce glare. 'Do you really think you're the only one who cares about what happens to Angeline?'

'It certainly seems that way to me.'

'Well, you're wrong! There might have been times when I didn't get along too well with my cousin, but I certainly don't want anything to happen to her. And I'll do whatever I can to help her if she's in serious trouble.'

'You've said that before,' Benedict replied, not looking in the least impressed by her outburst. 'But so far, you've done remarkably little to prove that you mean what you say.'

'I'm here in Istanbul, aren't I?'

'Because I virtually dragged you here.'

'Even if I'd never set eyes on you—and heaven knows, I wish that I hadn't!—I'd still have come,' Amy flung at him vehemently.

He looked completely unconvinced, which infuriated her even further.

'All right,' she yelled at him in a sudden burst of frustration, 'I'll do whatever I have to do to make you believe that I really want to help Angeline. I'll even sit by that phone for twenty-four hours a day, waiting for this ransom demand that you think's going to come. And if you want to sit right beside me, then that's fine. It'll be a complete waste of time, but it's obviously quite useless trying to convince you of that.'

As soon as she had said it, she wished that she had kept her mouth shut. She certainly *didn't* want to be stuck in the same room with him for the next couple of days. She had rashly agreed to do just that, though, and she didn't quite see how she could get out of it. If she tried to tell him that she had changed her mind, he would simply accuse her all over again of not caring what happened to Angeline. And she was getting very tired of hearing that accusation.

Amy opened her case and muttered balefully under her breath as she shovelled her clothes into drawers and cupboards. She pointedly ignored Benedict's own bag, which still stood by the door. He needn't think that she was going to do his unpacking as well!

'You can unlock the door now,' she informed him, with a bad-tempered scowl.

He fingered the key thoughtfully. 'You're not going to run away?'

'From what?' she said scornfully. 'You? I'm not afraid of you, you know. It's just that you're about the last person on earth I want to share a room with.'

'The feeling's mutual,' Benedict said coolly. 'You've a lot of traits that I find extremely unattractive. By choice, I'd sooner not spend any time with you at all.'

The man certainly knew how to be totally insulting. Amy shot a malevolent look at him, and then deliberately turned her back on him.

The next couple of days promised to be just about the most unpleasant that she had ever spent.

CHAPTER THREE

BENEDICT unlocked the door, and left the key in the lock, which made Amy feel very slightly safer. At least she could make a run for it if anything happened that she didn't like.

Not that she was expecting any real problems concerning Benedict's behaviour towards her. He had made it very clear that he wasn't interested in her in any way. He only needed her around because she was his one link with Angeline.

She sat on the edge of the bed and watched him as he unpacked. His movements were deft and neat, as if he were used to looking after himself and had done this kind of thing dozens of times before. She found herself wondering about his personal life. There didn't seem to be any wife in the background, and from something he had said earlier, she had the feeling that there hadn't been too many long-term relationships, either. That was odd for a man who had to be in his early thirties.

Amy's gaze slid over him, taking in small details that she had missed before. The stern line of his mouth, as if he rarely found life amusing; the thickness of the black lashes that fringed his dark eyes; the uncompromising expression on the strong lines of his face; and the powerful, supple body that she somehow found rather intimidating.

He suddenly glanced up at her and she instantly felt herself going bright red. Furious at being caught

studying him so intently, she got quickly to her feet
and walked over to the window.

'Are we going down to dinner soon?' she asked
abruptly. 'I'm starving.'

'I'm going to ring down and ask for dinner to be
sent up to our room. That way, we won't miss any
phone-call that might come.'

Amy stared at him incredulously. 'Do you mean
that we've got to spend every minute of our stay in
Istanbul right here, in this room?'

'That seems the best way of making sure that we
get any message that Angeline tries to send.'

'You can simply ask to be paged,' she said a little
impatiently.

'They might forget. Or not bother. I don't want to
risk that.'

'And *I* don't want to spend the next couple of days
sitting here staring at you!' she retorted.

Benedict shrugged. 'Then read a book. Or watch
television.'

'The programmes will all be in Turkish!'

He gave an uninterested shrug, as if to say that that
wasn't his problem. 'I'm going to take a shower,' he
said, and disappeared into the adjoining bathroom.

Amy gave a frustrated sigh, and stared out of the
window. The sun was sinking fast now, leaving a
golden-red glow in the sky. The dying rays of the sun
glinted on the waters of the Golden Horn, the elegant
minarets of the mosques etched their thin black
shadows against the brilliant colours of the sunset,
and lights began to shine softly from the buildings all
around.

The streets were still packed and noisy. Istanbul
seemed to be a city that was constantly on the move.

People going to and from work, tourists tramping round the mosques and palaces and bazaars, late shoppers browsing around for bargains; Amy looked down at them enviously. She wished she could be down in the crowded streets with them. Anywhere, in fact, except stuck here in this hotel-room with Benedict Kane.

He came out of the bathroom a few minutes later, his hair looking almost black now that it was wet and slicked back. He was wearing clean jeans and a shirt, but despite his casual clothes, there wasn't anything informal about his manner.

He went over to the phone and picked it up. Then he looked at her. 'What do you want to eat?'

A few minutes ago, she had been starving. Quite suddenly, though, her appetite had vanished and she felt as if it would take a major effort to swallow even a few mouthfuls of food.

'Oh—I'll have some fish,' she said, although without any trace of enthusiasm. At least a light meal shouldn't cause the tense muscles of her stomach too many problems. 'I'll take a shower while we're waiting for it to be sent up.'

She grabbed a towel and a handful of clean clothes, then scurried into the bathroom. She didn't know why she suddenly wanted to get away from Benedict. She only knew that there were times when her nervous system went into overdrive when he was around—and this was one of them!

Once the bathroom door was closed behind her, she felt slightly better. She stripped off, twisted the pale blonde strands of her hair into a knot on top of her head, and then stepped under the shower.

The water came out in a tepid trickle, and she had to stand under it for ages before she felt properly clean. She didn't mind, though. It meant that she could postpone the moment when she would have to go back into the other room and face Benedict again.

You don't have to do *any* of this, she reminded herself, as she rubbed herself dry. You can go down to Reception and demand another room. You can even catch the next flight back to England if you want to.

Then she gave a resigned sigh. She couldn't actually do either of those things. Not until this mystery concerning Angeline had finally been cleared up.

She wriggled into a pair of clean jeans, pulled on a T-shirt, and released her hair from its knot, shaking her head so that the silky golden strands cascaded back down to her shoulders. Then she stared at herself in the mirror.

Her green eyes gazed warily back at her. She looked defensive and on edge, and she didn't like that. With an effort, she fixed her mouth into a confident smile. Then she walked purposefully back into the other room.

She discovered that their dinner had just arrived. Benedict was removing the covers from the plates, and setting them out on a small table.

'Are you ready to eat?' he asked, glancing up at her as she came in.

Amy nodded, and sat down. She began to pick at her fish, which was served with lemon and parsley, and a fresh salad. Benedict was eating lamb mixed with a variety of vegetables. There were bowls of fresh fruit salad for dessert.

Her appetite slowly returned, and she managed to eat everything that was in front of her. They finished

the meal with cups of sweet, strong coffee, then piled
the empty plates back on to the trolley which Amy
pushed outside the door, to be collected later by room-
service.

Neither of them had said a word all through the
meal. Amy had expected the prolonged silence to
become thoroughly uncomfortable, but to her surprise that hadn't happened.

When she went back into the room, she found that
Benedict had walked over to the window and was now
staring out. He looked as if he was entirely wrapped
up in his own thoughts. Amy had the distinct feeling
that, for the moment at least, he had forgotten that
she was even there.

He was probably thinking of Angeline, she told
herself, with a wrinkling of her nose. Her cousin must
have pulled out all the stops to get a man like Benedict
Kane into such an emotional twist! For just an instant, Amy felt unexpectedly jealous. She doubted if
she was ever going to have that sort of effect on a
man. She sometimes felt that she was just a paler
version of Angeline—less glitz and glamour, less sex-
appeal, less of everything that it took to make a man
forget about everything except the existence of one
particular woman.

Amy found herself surprised—and rather disturbed—by the way her thoughts were running. Had
Benedict been right all along? she wondered with a
darkening frown. *Was* she jealous of her cousin?

No, she certainly wasn't, she tried to convince
herself. Then she looked at Benedict again. From the
closed, withdrawn expression on his face, she could
tell that he was still quite oblivious to her presence.

With a small jolt of shock, she realised that she didn't like that.

Don't be stupid, she told herself uneasily. It's to your advantage that he's completely indifferent towards you. You don't want him breathing down your neck all the time, do you? Pawing you? Trying to jump on you in the middle of the night?

She stared at the familiar outline of his face; the dark glow of his eyes. Her nerve-ends gave a small jump, her heart thumped hard and painfully, and then she shivered. Quickly, Amy turned away. What on earth was happening to her? she wondered with a touch of panic. She felt really odd. As if something inside of her had suddenly changed.

Benedict's voice broke into her confused thoughts, making her jump. 'It's been a long day,' he said crisply. 'Perhaps we ought to try and get some sleep.'

'That—that sounds like a good idea,' Amy got out in a voice that didn't sound at all like her own. 'I'll—I'll get undressed first, if you like.'

She rummaged around in the drawer for her night things. Then, for the second time that day, she fled into the safety of the bathroom.

She closed the door behind her, locked it, and then slumped against it for a minute, breathing unevenly. Then she walked over to the mirror and took another look at her reflection.

She was alarmed to find that she didn't look like the same girl who had stared at herself earlier. There were bright red patches of colour on her cheeks, an almost feverish brightness to her eyes, and her lips looked rather red and full, as if she had been biting them.

Amy ran an unsteady hand through the pale gold silk of her hair. 'What on earth's wrong with me?' she muttered in bewilderment. 'Some kind of illness? But I don't feel sick—just very odd! Anyway, I haven't been here long enough to pick up some local virus.'

She tried to think straight. When had it started? When she had been looking at Benedict, she realised, with a quickening thump of her pulses. But all these odd symptoms couldn't possibly have anything to do with him! She didn't *like* him, she reminded herself. In fact, there had been times when she had positively hated him. She didn't want to be here with him, and she would be quite happy if she never saw him again.

Except that that wasn't quite the truth. With something very like fear, she slowly realised that she would mind very much if she never saw him again.

This is crazy! she muttered in bewilderment. Until yesterday morning, I didn't even know he existed. We've done nothing except argue and get on each other's nerves. It doesn't make sense to feel anything for him except extreme dislike. I *can't* feel anything else.

She ran the cold tap and splashed the water over her face several times, trying to cool down the hot spots that still flared on her cheeks. Her breathing, which had been quick and uneven, slowed down a little, and she finally felt as if she was getting some kind of self-control back again.

You're tired after the long journey and overwrought because of this mysterious business with Angeline, she reasoned with herself. Under those sort of circumstances, anyone would feel rather odd. It's got absolutely nothing to do with Benedict Kane!

She told herself that several times, in a very firm voice. She had just reached the point where she had almost believed it when there was a sharp rap on the door, and the sound of Benedict's voice sent her heart thundering away all over again.

'You've been in there a long time,' he said. 'Are you all right?'

'Fine,' she croaked. 'I'm just—just washing and cleaning my teeth.'

She ran the taps, trying to make it sound as if she were doing just that. She even gave her teeth a half-hearted scrub, but all the time she was wondering how much longer she could lurk in the safety of the bathroom.

Not more than a couple of minutes, she decided with a heavy sigh. She had better get undressed and go back to the bedroom before he became too suspicious. She didn't want to do anything that would make him look at her too closely. He might see far more than she wanted him to see!

She scrambled out of her jeans and T-shirt, and pulled on the old, baggy nightshirt that she usually slept in. It was comfortable, but that was about all that could be said for it. It was probably the unsexiest piece of nightwear that Benedict Kane had ever seen. Wearing something like this at night was definitely one way of making sure that he remained completely indifferent to her as a female!

And was that what she wanted? Yes! she told herself fervently. That was *absolutely* what she wanted. She needed to be able to merge into the background, be completely unnoticeable, until she had got over this small piece of madness.

And she would get over it, she instructed herself grimly. She didn't know how it had ever happened in the first place, but it most certainly wasn't going to last. A good night's sleep should cure it. In the morning, she would wake up with a clear head and be able to see this for a piece of nonsense brought on by tiredness and anxiety.

With that decided, she opened the door and marched out of the bathroom.

At once, she was confronted with an unnervingly close view of Benedict. He was standing in the middle of the room, watching her as she emerged from the bathroom.

He looked taller, broader, darker, more intimidating, more—oh, more male than he had any right to be! Amy told herself angrily, her frayed nerves only adding to her edgy irritability.

'It doesn't seem likely that we'll be getting any phone-calls this late in the evening, so we might as well both get some sleep,' he said.

'Fine,' she snapped back at him. 'The bathroom's free, if you want to use it.'

And she hoped that he would be in there for a *very* long time. With any luck, by the time he came out, she would be asleep. As far as she was concerned, she just wanted to get through this night as quickly as possible—and preferably in a state of unconsciousness! In the morning, everything would be different. She had managed to totally convince herself of that. Things would be back to normal. They *had* to be, she told herself, fighting back another wave of panic, because if they weren't . . .

'You look rather flushed,' Benedict remarked, with a small frown. 'You're not coming down with some illness, are you?'

'Certainly not,' Amy said, making a huge effort to force the colour from her face. 'I wouldn't do anything as inconvenient as that,' she added, with quite unnecessary sarcasm. 'I know that you don't have any time for illness. Or for anything that would interfere with your search for Angeline.'

'It would certainly be a nuisance if you became ill,' he agreed coolly.

'I'm not ill!' she hissed at him. 'In fact, I'm perfectly healthy. The water was rather hot when I washed, that was all. That's why my face looks flushed.'

He didn't look entirely convinced. His dark gaze raked over her very sharply, as if trying to get right inside her head and find out exactly what was going on. Amy briefly closed her eyes and made a huge effort to block him out. He was *not* going to know what she was thinking. She would rather die than have him know all the crazy thoughts that had been running through her head tonight!

'Why don't you go into the bathroom and get ready for bed?' she said tightly, just wanting him to go away, even if it were only for a few minutes.

'There's not much point,' he replied casually. 'I'm going to sleep in my clothes.'

'You'd be more comfortable in pyjamas.'

'I never wear them.'

'Oh,' she said in a very strangled voice. Then, realising that she was over-reacting, she somehow managed to get some control over her disintegrating nerves. 'I really don't care *what* you wear to sleep in.

Just don't disturb me. I'm very tired, and I'm going straight to sleep.'

Amy flung herself down on her own bed and pointedly turned her back on him. A few moments later, she closed her eyes. Despite what she had said to Benedict, though, she knew that there wasn't the slightest chance of her getting any sleep.

She was certainly right about that, at least. An hour later, she was still wide awake, and all her muscles ached from the strain of trying to lie perfectly still, pretending to be soundly asleep. She could hear the sound of Benedict's quiet, even breathing, and resentment began to churn around inside her. He had barged into her life and turned everything completely upside down, and now he was going to sleep peacefully all night while she couldn't even manage to doze off for half an hour. It simply wasn't fair!

She rolled over and glared at him in the semi-darkness. He was sprawled out on the bed, eyes closed and looking totally relaxed. He had kicked off his shoes, but was still wearing jeans and an unbuttoned shirt. Amy pulled a face. She supposed she ought to be grateful that he hadn't insisted on sleeping naked. Or had he just said that because he knew that her reaction would amuse him?

If this man had a sense of humour at all—and she wasn't at all sure yet that he did—then she was sure that it had to be very warped. He didn't behave like any other man she had ever known. She was never absolutely sure when he was being serious, or if that dark light in the depths of his eyes meant that he was silently laughing at her. She could never guess what he was going to do or say, and she didn't like that. In fact, there were very few things that she *did* like about him. That was what made her odd reaction to him earlier so impossible to understand.

You need to forget about that! she instructed herself sternly. It was just a short spell of madness brought on by tiredness and worry. In the morning, you'll remember what happened, and laugh at yourself for behaving in such a crazy, stupid way.

Except that it still seemed a very long time until morning. And if she didn't manage to get some sleep she was going to feel just as tired, which might mean that she would still feel exactly the same. And that was definitely something to worry about!

Amy thumped the pillow to fluff it up, tossed restlessly a couple of times, and then let out an audible sigh.

'Having problems getting to sleep?' enquired Benedict's voice, drifting softly out of the semi-darkness.

She nearly jumped right off the bed. She had thought he was so soundly asleep that nothing would wake him up.

'You should have warned me that you suffered from insomnia,' he went on. 'I might not have been so insistent on sharing a room with you!'

'I don't suffer from insomnia,' Amy insisted indignantly. 'I just have problems sleeping in a strange bed.' And with a strange man only a few feet away, she nearly added, only just stopping herself in time. 'On top of that, it's very noisy outside,' she added defensively. 'Don't the people in this city ever sleep?'

'I expect the people who live and work here keep fairly normal hours. But the city's also bursting with tourists, and they want to pack as much as they can into the time they spend here. Why waste part of your holiday doing something boring like sleeping?'

It unnerved her to hear his voice murmuring gently in the darkness. And it sounded quite different, free from the terse and often short-tempered tones he used during the day. For the first time since she had met him—and it was difficult to believe that that had only been a day and a half ago—he seemed quite relaxed.

Amy found herself wondering if this was the way he sounded when he spoke to Angeline. Then, an instant later, she was shocked rigid by a bolt of pure jealousy which shot through her from head to toe.

Panic rolled over her. I don't *care* how he sounds when he talks to Angeline, she insisted to herself frantically. It doesn't matter to me, it isn't important, I don't even want to think about it!

She squeezed her eyes shut very tight. If only she could go to sleep! She just wanted this nightmarish day to come to an end.

To her utter relief, Benedict didn't say anything more. His breathing became very quiet again, but she wasn't fooled this time. He was no more asleep than she was. She kept her own eyes closed and lay very still, trying to force her tense muscles to relax. And, after a couple of very long hours, she eventually fell asleep.

When Amy opened her eyes again, it was daylight. For those first couple of seconds, she couldn't figure out where she was. Confusedly, she rubbed her eyes, which still felt heavy. Then the room gradually slid into focus and she suddenly remembered everything much more clearly than she actually wanted to.

With a stifled groan, she sat up. She was in Istanbul, with Benedict Kane.

To her relief, she found that she could say his name with no more than a very slight twitching of her nerve-ends. She looked round at the other twin bed, and that relief grew when she found it was empty. She supposed that he was either in the bathroom, or had already dressed and gone down for an early breakfast.

Amy flipped the pale, tangled skeins of her hair back from her face, stretched her cramped limbs, then hauled herself off the bed and padded over to the window.

The streets below were already packed with people and traffic. The sun was shining down out of a clear blue sky, shops were open for business, boats plied up and down the Bosporus, and Istanbul braced itself for another hectic, noisy day.

Amy was bracing herself for something completely different. She was going to have to spend today cooped up in this room with Benedict, and the prospect didn't thrill her in the least. In fact, to be perfectly frank, it made her extremely nervous even to think about it.

You're not tired any more, she tried to reassure herself. You shouldn't have any problems this morning. What happened yesterday was just something that was rather freakish.

She began to relax a little when she realised that she could think about Benedict without getting too agitated. She hadn't had a lot of sleep, but it looked as if she had had enough to cure her of all the peculiar tricks her mind had tried to play on her last night.

With growing confidence, Amy rummaged in the cupboard, pulling out clean undies, a pair of white cotton trousers and a thin T-shirt. After a long, hot shower, she would feel completely like herself again and ready to cope with anything—even Benedict Kane.

She was actually humming softly under her breath as she finally headed towards the bathroom. Just as she was about to waltz inside, though, the door to the bedroom opened, and Benedict came in.

Amy turned to face him, her eyes calm and her mouth relaxed but not quite smiling. Polite but distant; that was going to be her attitude towards him today. In fact, she thought that that would be a good—and safe—attitude to adopt for the whole of the rest of their stay in Istanbul.

However, as soon as she actually looked at him, things began to fall apart. Oh, heavens, how could she possibly have forgotten how tall he was? How physically overwhelming? Or how his dark eyes bored so deeply into her, as if they could see right inside her head?

She found she was breathing heavily, as if she had been doing some hard physical exercises. With a huge effort, she stopped gulping air into her lungs. Act normally! she told herself in growing panic. If you don't, he'll suspect something, and that really will be disastrous!

To her relief, though, he only glanced at her for a couple of moments, and then he looked away again. Part of her was piqued that he was so uninterested in her, but for the most part she was utterly relieved that he was so indifferent. It meant that her secret was safe for a while longer, and time was what she desperately needed right now. Time to find a way of coping with this. Time to think of a way of disguising everything she was feeling, so that he would never know what sort of effect he was having on her.

And what sort of effect *was* he having? Amy didn't know; it was quite impossible to describe it. She just knew that it was absolutely unlike anything that she had ever felt before—and that she desperately wanted it to go away again!

Benedict came further into the room, and she instinctively backed away. He noticed her edgy retreat and his mouth immediately set into an irritable line.

'There's no need to behave like that. I've already told you that I've no intention of laying a single finger on you.'

'I'm not—I didn't think——' Amy somehow got control of herself and managed to get out a complete sentence. 'It's just that I'm not dressed,' she said defensively.

Benedict almost looked amused. 'You could walk right through the streets of Istanbul in that nightshirt, and you'd have absolutely nothing to worry about. The damned thing's more effective than a chastity belt. Believe me, no one's going to try and touch you while you're wearing it!'

She scowled at him. 'It isn't that bad!'

One of his dark eyebrows gently rose. 'Take a look in the mirror some time.' Then, before she could fling another reply back at him, he went on, 'Do you mind if I use the shower first? I've been out running, and it's already fairly hot out there.'

Amy's own pale blonde eyebrows shot up. 'You've been running? In Istanbul? I should think you were bumping into someone every couple of steps!'

'The main streets were pretty crowded,' he admitted. 'But some of the side-streets were emptier. Although I did get a few odd looks,' he added drily.

'I don't think that early morning jogging's caught on here yet.'

'I didn't know you were a fitness freak. Do you do this kind of thing every morning?'

'I'm not a fitness freak, and I only go running when I've been forced to sit around in one place for too long, and need to stretch my muscles.'

And very powerful and well-shaped muscles they looked, Amy noted with a definite gulp.

'If you want to use the bathroom first, that's OK with me,' she said rather too quickly. Anything to get him out of the room for a few minutes. *Nothing* had improved or altered since last night, and she badly needed some time on her own to rethink the situation.

Benedict disappeared into the bathroom. She let out a massive sigh of relief and slumped on to the bed. For a couple of minutes she just lay there, staring up at the ceiling. Her mind wouldn't seem to work, and her body kept gently quivering, as if someone were running a slight electric shock through it.

Finally, she forced herself to sit up and think clearly, although the last was a lot harder to do than the first. Make some sort of plan, she told herself. Lay down guidelines and then stick to them. That's the only way you're going to be able to get through the next couple of days.

All right, she decided, gritting her teeth, let's start with the obvious. One: spend as little time with Benedict Kane as possible. Not easy, when he doesn't seem to want to let you out of his sight, but grab every opportunity to get away from him. Two: don't look at him or even *think* about him, unless it's absolutely necessary. Three: keep telling yourself that these freakish feelings won't last. You'll wake up one morning, and they'll have vanished as quickly and mysteriously as they came.

She felt slightly better now that she had a plan of action. And perhaps Angeline would turn up today, apologising for sending that silly letter and assuring them that, whatever trouble she had got herself into, it was all over now—she had sorted it out, and they could all go home.

Benedict ambled out of the bathroom at that point, dressed in jeans and a clean sweatshirt, and rubbing his damp hair with a towel. Amy carefully avoided looking at him.

'Can I shower now?' she asked.

'Go ahead.'

She gathered up her clothes, toilet bag and a towel, and sidled towards the bathroom door. Just as she reached it, though, Benedict brushed past her.

'Hang on a second; I'll turn on the shower for you. It's being rather temperamental this morning. You have to jiggle around with it for a while before it runs hot.'

He had been so close as he had moved by her that she had actually smelt the fresh scent of his skin. Worse than that, though, for just a moment she had felt her hand momentarily move towards him.

Amy closed her eyes. Oh, God, she had wanted to *touch* him.

This was really sick, she told herself. To feel like this about a perfect stranger. And a stranger that she didn't even like!

Benedict re-emerged from the bathroom. 'The shower's running hot now. Better get under it before it goes cold again,' he advised.

Amy muttered something totally incoherent under her breath, bolted into the bathroom, and slammed the door shut behind her.

This was getting completely out of hand, she told herself in pure panic. What on earth was she going to do? Another couple of days of this and men in white coats were going to have to come and take her away!

She pulled off her nightshirt and got under the shower. The hot water beating down on her calmed her just a little. Try and work out what's happened, she instructed herself. Once you understand it, perhaps you can do something about it.

But how could she possibly understand something that was so inexplicable? Here was a man whom she actively disliked, and yet every time he looked at her, something inside of her began to shake. He only had to come near, and she wanted to reach out and touch him. None of it made the slightest sense—but it certainly scared her half to death!

She spent ages under the shower. Her skin was beginning to wrinkle by the time she reluctantly turned it off and began to dry herself.

Very, very slowly, she pulled on her clothes. She wanted to put off for as long as possible the moment when she was going to have to go back out there and see him; speak to him; try to act normal, when the way she felt inside wasn't normal at all!

When she finally left the bathroom, her feet dragging as she forced them to carry her back into the bedroom, Benedict shot a dry look at her.

'Do you always spend this much time in the bathroom? Every time you disappear in there, you seem to stay there longer and longer. If you carry on like this, you're not going to come out at all in a couple of days!'

'I—I just felt like a long shower,' she mumbled. She edged her way over to the window and looked out. She really longed to be out there in those hot, crowded streets. She could get lost in the throng of people—try to forget for a short time that a man called Benedict Kane even existed.

'I think I need to go out for a while,' she said in a rush. 'Just for a walk—to get some fresh air.'

'You need to stay here,' he said at once. 'In case Angeline tries to get in touch.'

'*You* went out this morning,' Amy reminded him, her voice taking on a sharp edge because she really was quite desperate to get out of this room, even if it were only for half an hour.

'I'm not the one that Angeline sent that letter to,' he reminded her.

'Damn Angeline!' she said with sudden vehemence. 'I wish she were a thousand miles away from here.'

Benedict's mouth immediately set into a hard, grim line. 'You've already made it perfectly clear how you feel about your cousin. Thank God I turned up at your shop on the same morning that her letter arrived. If I hadn't been there, you'd probably have torn it up, thrown it away, and just forgotten about it.'

'I would not!' Amy denied indignantly. 'And perhaps you wouldn't be so eager to help my cousin if you knew her a little better.'

'What exactly do you mean by that?' he said tightly. But before she had a chance to reply, the telephone rang.

Amy jumped violently. The shrill sound echoed through the room, and she stared at the phone nervously.

'Answer it,' Benedict instructed in a taut voice. When she didn't move, he strode over to her and gave her an impatient shake. 'Pick it up and answer it!' he repeated, his dark eyes blazing down at her.

Her hand visibly trembling, she reached out and picked up the receiver.

'Hello?' she said in almost a whisper.

A man's voice, slightly muffled, echoed down the line.

'Is that Amy Stewart?'

'Yes, it is.'

'Then listen very carefully if you want to see your cousin again. We have her and she's safe at the moment, but she might very well get hurt if you do anything stupid, like going to the police. Understand?'

Amy had to cough to clear her constricted throat before she could answer him. 'Yes,' she finally got out, in a cracked tone.

'It's very important that no one becomes suspicious,' the man's voice went on. 'So we want you to act as if you're here on holiday. Go and see the sights. Take snapshots, buy postcards and souvenirs. When we're satisfied that you're behaving sensibly, and that you haven't involved any of the authorities, we'll be in touch again.'

'How?' she said quickly. 'Will you ring me here, at the hotel?'

'We might telephone, or we might find some other way of getting a message to you. Just remember that we'll be watching you all the time; so make sure that you follow our instructions exactly.'

'Is Angeline all right?' Amy asked urgently.

'She's fine—for now.'

'Can I see her? Speak to her?'

The line went dead in her hand. She stared at the phone for several moments, and then slowly put it down.

'What did they say?' Benedict demanded tautly.

She had almost forgotten that he was there. With an effort, she pulled herself together and then repeated the conversation, almost word for word.

Benedict's face darkened. 'So I was right,' he said grimly. 'Someone has snatched Angeline.'

'What are we going to do?' Amy asked numbly. She was still finding it incredibly hard to take all of this in. Right up until the moment when the phone had rung, she had believed that Angeline would cheerfully bounce in and apologise for sending such a frantic letter. Her cousin loved being over-dramatic and exaggerating everything that happened to her. Only, this time, she hadn't exaggerated at all. She was in deadly serious trouble, and relying on Amy to get her safely out of it.

'For now, we do exactly as they've instructed,' Benedict said, his features setting into a black expression. She guessed that he hated being so helpless, being able to do nothing except go along with the kidnapper's demands.

Amy gave a small shiver. Suddenly, everything had changed, become much more dangerous.

She didn't even feel relieved that she didn't have to cope with it on her own—that she had Benedict Kane to give help and advice. Somehow, that only added to the aura of danger that surrounded this whole affair.

CHAPTER FOUR

AMY paced restlessly over to the window, and stared out. Somewhere out there was her cousin, Angeline. She was alone, certainly very frightened, and probably wondering if anyone was ever going to rescue her.

She swung back to face Benedict. She found that she could look at him quite easily now, with no more than a slightly faster-than-usual thumping of her pulses.

'I think that we ought to go to the police,' she said in a very clear voice. 'This is more than we can handle. We need someone who knows how to deal with this kind of thing.'

'No,' Benedict said flatly. 'I'm not going to do anything that will put Angeline in any kind of danger. And I won't allow you to do it, either.'

'I think we're putting her in more danger by *not* going to the police,' Amy argued stubbornly. 'They've got experience of this kind of thing. They'll be able to advise us; they'll know what to do.'

'They might also get Angeline killed, if the kidnappers find out that the very first thing we've done is to disobey their instructions,' he said in a grim voice. 'I'm not willing to risk that.'

'We might be putting her even more at risk by trying to deal with this alone. I'm no good at this sort of thing. I don't like intrigue and I hate danger.' Amy brushed quickly at her eyes, which were suddenly prickling ominously. 'If I mess this up and something happens to Angeline, then it's all going to be *my* fault. I couldn't live with that. I really couldn't.'

Benedict looked at her without much sympathy. 'And that's why you want to involve the police? So you can blame *them* if something goes wrong? You think that that'll let you walk away with a clear conscience? You can tell yourself that you weren't the one who messed it up? Well, it doesn't work like that, Amy,' he said, fixing his dark gaze on her. 'You're involved, and you're going to stay involved. If things look like getting out of hand then we might have to call in the police, but only as a very last resort. Angeline's relying on you to get her out of this safely, and that's exactly what you're going to do.'

'I don't think I can,' she said, a frightened tremor in her voice. 'Look, I thought Angeline sent me that letter because she was going through some sort of emotional crisis, and she couldn't face it on her own. She has them quite regularly, and she always wants someone to hold her hand and see her through them. Or I thought that it might even be a hoax. She likes playing tricks on people, she gets a real kick out of it. But this——' She gave a huge shiver. 'This is different. This is for real. And I can't handle it.'

Benedict walked over until he was standing only inches in front of her. His hands gripped the top of her arms and she was starkly aware of the warmth of his body, the light fanning of his breath against her face, and the too-fast beating of his own pulses.

'You're going to handle it,' he told her in a harsh tone. 'You're not running out on Angeline, you little coward.'

His words hit her hard. They were more effective than a physical blow. Amy stopped shivering, and her eyes changed, their colour becoming darker and more intense.

'Let go of me,' she said in a low voice.

He instantly released her. She rubbed her arms, as if trying to get rid of the imprint of his fingers. Then, very gradually, she straightened her shoulders and lifted her head.

'I still think we should go to the police. But all right, we'll try and tackle this on our own, if you really think Angeline will be safer that way. Remember this, though. I'm going to the authorities straight away, if things look as if they're going wrong. And I'm not going to take orders from you; not any more. We'll do things *my* way, or not at all.'

Benedict growled something under his breath, obviously not liking this sudden change in her.

Amy found that she felt much better now that she was actually standing up to him. She seemed to have been falling further and further under this man's influence ever since he had first walked into her shop, with everything threatening to get completely out of hand. Well, things were going to change! He kept telling her that she was responsible for Angeline's safety, and so she was going to *be* responsible. That meant taking decisions on her own, and sticking to them. It also meant not being over-awed by him in any way, or letting him get to her. She took a deep breath. That definitely wouldn't be easy! But perhaps she could manage it if she kept telling herself that she was doing it for Angeline—that her cousin's safety, perhaps even her life, was at stake.

'Right,' she said in a much crisper voice, 'I've already decided what we're going to do today.'

Benedict looked as if he definitely didn't like this change in her, but he didn't interrupt her, although his eyes began to gleam with a warning light. Amy ignored it, though.

'We're going to follow the kidnappers' instructions as far as we can. I'm going to act like a tourist, visit some of the sights of Istanbul, and let them see that I'm not acting suspiciously in any way. I hope that'll make them get in touch again fairly soon. When they do that, I'll decide what I'm going to do next.' She picked up her bag and rummaged through it. 'I'll go to the bank first and change some money,' she went on. 'Then I'll pick up a guide-book and try to find my way to a couple of the more popular tourist spots. A lot of people should be heading for the same places, so I shouldn't get lost.'

'No, you won't get lost, because I'm coming with you,' Benedict told her. 'And I've an excellent sense of direction.'

'I'm going on my own,' Amy said at once.

He shook his head. 'You're not going anywhere on your own.'

'These people, whoever they are, are expecting to see just me. If they catch sight of you, then everything could go wrong. You could be putting Angeline in real danger, and you keep saying that's the one thing you don't want to do!'

'And if I don't go with you, then *you* could be in danger,' Benedict pointed out. 'We don't know who these people are or how much we can trust them. I brought you here, which unfortunately makes me responsible for you. I'm staying close to you until this is all over.'

'You did not bring me here,' Amy said angrily. 'You booked my ticket on the plane, that was all. I'd have come even if I'd never met you.'

'So you keep telling me,' he said coolly, his tone telling her very clearly that he didn't believe her. 'But the fact remains that I have to get you, as well as Angeline, safely back home. And that means, like it or not, that you don't go anywhere without me.'

'Oh, this is ridiculous!' she said furiously, stamping her foot in frustration. 'I'm over twenty-one, and you don't have any kind of legal hold over me. That means I can go where I please and do whatever I want.'

'You certainly can—once this is all over. Until then, wherever you go, I go.'

Her green eyes flashed at him. 'You still don't trust me, do you?' she accused. 'You think I'm going to run off, abandon Angeline just when she needs me.'

His own gaze rested on her assessingly. 'I think that's perfectly possible,' he replied calmly, outraging her still further. 'That's one more reason why I don't intend to let you out of my sight.'

Green and dark eyes locked together for a few more seconds, one pair blazing angrily, the other more composed but still glinting with an unexpectedly dangerous light.

Amy was the first one to look away. 'This is stupid,' she muttered. 'Why are we behaving like this, when we ought to be thinking about Angeline?'

'I don't know,' he said with unexpected honesty. 'But perhaps we should try to keep the fighting down to a minimum over the next couple of days. It's simply making everything much more difficult.'

'That's fine by me. But I think it would help if you made an effort to be less overbearing.'

Benedict looked genuinely surprised. 'I don't think I'm overbearing.'

She let out a huge snort. 'Then I'd be interested to hear how you *would* describe the way you've behaved over the last couple of days!'

He gave a slightly impatient shrug. 'We're beginning to argue again, and it's getting us nowhere. There are far more important things we ought to be discussing.'

'Such as?'

'Exactly where we're going today. You've told me that you want to go to the bank. I suggest that, after that, we head for the Topkapi Palace. We've been told to act like genuine tourists, and that's the place that most tourists head for first when they arrive in Istanbul.'

'*I've* been told to behave like a tourist,' Amy reminded him. 'The kidnappers don't even know that you're here. If they're watching me, though, they'll soon see you. What excuse are you going to give for being here?'

'I'll think of something,' Benedict promised vaguely. He glanced at his watch. 'Let's get going. Quite apart from anything else, I've had more than enough of this hotel-room.'

Amy was quite willing to agree with him on that! She slung her bag over her shoulder and followed him out of the room.

A hot blast of sunshine hit them as they left the hotel. The streets were as noisy and crowded as ever, as Benedict shouldered his way through the crowds, heading towards the bank and leaving Amy to trudge along in his wake. Voices chattered all around them in a dozen different languages; cars, trucks and taxis

toiled slowly along the jammed roads, horns blaring
and engines revving up, although without any real
hope of moving any faster; shopkeepers haggled over
their prices with customers, and perspiring groups of
tourists tried to work out in which direction they
should be heading.

When Amy finally reached the bank, there was a
long queue, and it was nearly three quarters of an
hour later before she finally emerged with a wad of
Turkish lira stuffed into her bag. She felt slightly better
now that she had some money of her own. Not quite
so dependent on Benedict. And she was going to insist
on paying for her share of their room as soon as they
got back to the hotel.

'Where now?' she asked.

'The Topkapi Palace,' he replied briefly. 'It's the
obvious place to visit first, if we're pretending to be
tourists.'

Amy glanced round at the confusing maze of streets.
'Do you have any idea which way to go?'

'Just follow me,' Benedict instructed, and set off
at a brisk pace.

Since he seemed to know where he was going, Amy
gave a short sigh and then hurried after him. She
nearly lost him several times as he disappeared in the
great mass of people that thronged the streets. Then
she would catch sight of his dark head again, the shape
of it somehow completely distinctive, and she would
scurry to catch up with him.

'How do you know where the Topkapi Palace is?'
she demanded rather breathlessly, as she fell into step
beside him.

'I looked at a map of Istanbul before we left the
hotel.'

'Most people who come here spend hours poring over maps, but they still get lost,' she pointed out.

'I never get lost,' Benedict replied calmly.

Amy gave a brief scowl. She almost wished that they would end up miles from the palace so that, just for once, he would have to admit that he had been wrong about something.

She could already see the great bulk of the church of Haghia Sophia, though, flanked by its four tall minarets, and with its massive dome solidly dominating the skyline. She knew that the church was close to the palace, which meant that Benedict's sense of direction had been annoyingly accurate.

A short while later, they reached the Topkapi Palace and walked through the first courtyard towards the Middle Gate, which was the main entrance. Just before they reached it, Benedict pointed out the fountain to the right of the gate.

'That's known as the executioner's fountain,' he told Amy, flicking through the guide book. 'The chief executioner used to wash his sword and his hands there, after he'd dispatched anyone whom the sultan considered to be a traitor.'

Amy raised her eyebrows. 'I can see this is going to be a really cheerful tour. Do you have any more interesting pieces of information like that?'

They walked through the arched entrance of the Middle Gate, and into the second courtyard. It was surrounded by porticoes, and crossed by footpaths that led in between bushes smothered with bright roses.

'The palace kitchens are over there,' Benedict said, pointing to the right. 'You might be interested in seeing them, if you like oriental porcelain.'

Amy looked at him with some impatience. 'I'm not really interested in any of this,' she retorted. 'If I were on holiday, then it would be fine; I'd have fun exploring every inch of this place. But I'm *not* on holiday. And all I keep thinking about right now is that someone's probably watching us. That man who phoned must be following us around, to check that we're doing exactly what he told us to do.' She glanced round nervously at the groups of people ambling casually through the courtyard. 'He could be just yards away and we wouldn't even know, because we don't know what he looks like.'

'There's every chance that he isn't following us at all,' Benedict said calmly. 'That could well have been just a threat, to make sure that we obeyed his instructions.'

'But you don't know that for certain.' Benedict simply shrugged, which made Amy really annoyed. 'I don't think you're taking this at all seriously,' she accused him.

His dark eyes immediately narrowed and his mouth set into a grim line. 'Believe me, I'm taking it very seriously. But there's absolutely nothing we can do until that man gets in touch with us again. So let's try to get through the next few hours without too many arguments, accusations or unpleasant scenes.'

'All right,' agreed Amy, in a more subdued tone. 'And I'm not deliberately trying to make things more difficult. It's just that I'm still finding this rather hard to cope with.'

'I know,' he said, with unexpected understanding. 'How about taking a look around the Harem? That might take your mind off our problems for a while.'

Amy very much doubted if anything was going to be able to do that! She trailed after him as he headed in that direction, though. She felt restless and wanted to keep on the move.

They had to join a guided tour, since visitors weren't allowed to wander through the Harem on their own. But they tagged on to the very end, and then lingered for a while in a room covered with beautiful tiles, letting the main group move some way ahead of them.

Amy and Benedict followed at a leisurely pace, through a small mosque with walls covered with more exquisitely patterned tiles, and then out into a courtyard that had wrought-iron lamps hanging on a colonnade down the middle. There were small rooms on either side, and Benedict nodded towards them with a very faint grin.

'These were the quarters of the black eunuchs. They were the guardians of the "sultan's greatest treasure".'

'In other words, his poor wives,' said Amy with some indignation. 'Cooped up here like prisoners, and never allowed to go out, see other people, or live normal lives.'

'They lived in great luxury,' Benedict pointed out.

'That hardly makes up for all the things they were never allowed to do. They must have been bored to death, with nothing to do all day except make themselves beautiful, in case the sultan decided he wanted one of them to share his bed!'

'Perhaps we'd better move on,' he said, almost smiling now. 'I don't think that this is the place to get involved in an argument on women's rights.'

Amy's eyes gleamed. 'You probably just feel uncomfortable because this is the eunuchs' quarters. I shouldn't think many men want to stay here for too long!'

He raised one eyebrow expressively, and then walked off. Amy grinned to herself, and then followed him.

They caught up with the main group in the apartments of the chief wives of the sultan. They moved on to the apartments of the Queen Mother, all the rooms sumptuously decorated and blazing with colour. Then they were in the part of the Harem that had been used by the sultan himself.

They stopped in front of a great white marble bath that had a grille set in front of it, to protect the sultans from attempts on their life while they bathed.

'They obviously didn't feel too secure even here, in the Harem,' Amy commented.

'Where someone has great power, there's always someone else wanting to take it away from them,' said Benedict. 'Intrigue, murder, plots and counterplots—their lives were never dull!'

'You sound slightly envious,' Amy said in surprise. 'Your life isn't dull, is it? Or do you just like the idea of having a harem?' she added, her green eyes suddenly gleaming.

'My life certainly hasn't been dull for the last couple of days,' Benedict said drily. 'And one woman at a time is quite enough for me. Sometimes too much, in fact!'

Amy wondered if he were talking about Angeline. Her cousin could certainly be hard to live with, at times. *Had* they lived together? she found herself wondering. On Benedict's own admission, they hadn't known each other for very long, but that didn't usually stop Angeline from plunging straight into a fairly intense relationship.

For the first time since they had left the hotel, she felt a ripple of jealousy running through her. Oh, no, she thought with a sinking feeling. Not again! She had thought she was over that. Ever since that phonecall this morning, she hadn't been able to think of anything except the very real danger that Angeline was in. Now, though, all the confused feelings of last night were beginning to creep back. With an effort, she tried to push them away; but they didn't want to go. There was something about this place—with its echoes of luxurious sensuality, memories of long nights of love or sheer lust, lives that were devoted solely to the arts of pleasure—that was beginning to make her feel slightly strange.

The tour party moved on, but Amy was reaching the stage where she could only take in fleeting and rather blurred images. A vaulted hall, fountains, crystal mirrors, splendid chandeliers and magnificent Chinese vases, decorated tiles and stained glass, paintings of flowers and fruit and geometric designs, and then something that she couldn't see but seemed to be vividly aware of, the ghosts of the scented, sensual, beautiful women who had lived here.

She was rather glad when they finally left the Harem, walking back out into the bright sunshine that filled the courtyard.

'Are you all right?' asked Benedict, looking at her and frowning slightly. 'You look a little odd.'

'I'm OK,' she said. 'At least, I am now. There was a rather funny atmosphere in there. Although I suppose that's not very surprising when you think of everything that must have happened in there over the centuries. All those women locked away for the pleasure of one man, and the only other men they ever saw were the eunuchs, who weren't quite men at all. There must have been so much frustrated desire, petty jealousies, power struggles when one favourite of the sultan was replaced by another. And all played out against that background of claustrophobic luxury.'

Benedict's dark gaze rested on her, and there was an expression in his eyes that she hadn't seen before. It was almost as if he were really looking at her for the very first time.

She thought that he was going to say something, and for just a moment she held her breath. Then he turned away rather suddenly, and began to walk over to the far side of the courtyard.

Amy followed more slowly. The sun beat down hotly on her head, and she felt very slightly dizzy, although she didn't think that it was from the heat. Benedict finally stopped and waited for her to catch up with him, and they walked on in silence for a few more yards.

'If you thought the Harem was luxurious, then perhaps you ought to visit the Treasury,' he suggested. 'Among other things, it houses the Topkapi dagger, and one of the largest diamonds in the world.'

At that particular moment, Amy wasn't particularly interested in jewels, no matter how large or famous they might be. But she wanted to get out of the sun, so she nodded in agreement.

'All right, let's take a look.'

She wandered through the first room without too much enthusiasm, looking at armour set with precious stones, weapons encrusted with more jewels, a magnificent throne, jade vases and gold plate.

In the second room, her green eyes did open rather wider as she gazed at the Topkapi dagger, studded with large emeralds and diamonds and set on a pearl-encrusted gold cushion.

'Like it?' murmured Benedict in her ear.

'The sultans certainly liked jewels,' she said, raising her eyebrows. 'It's all rather ostentatious, but I suppose it's not too hard to get used to all this glitz and glitter.'

'If you think this is ostentatious, come and look at the diamond in the next room,' he invited.

A minute later, she was staring through thick security glass at an eighty-six-carat diamond, surrounded by forty-nine smaller diamonds.

'Very nice,' Amy agreed. 'If you like diamonds.'

'I thought all women were supposed to like diamonds.'

She looked at him scornfully. 'Do you really believe that old cliché?'

Amusement shone briefly in his dark eyes. 'I don't think many women would refuse a diamond, if one were offered to them. But it's certainly the wrong stone for you. You need emeralds, to match your eyes.'

'I don't want diamonds *or* emeralds,' Amy said tartly. 'And I'm getting rather tired of staring at all these jewels. They're making my eyes ache.'

She marched out of the Treasury, not even looking to see if Benedict was following her. It was early afternoon by now, she was tired and hungry, and she was beginning to feel as if this was yet another day that was stretching on forever.

'I've seen all of the palace that I want to see,' she said in a rather abrupt voice, when Benedict finally caught up with her. 'Can we go now?'

'Perhaps we could get something to eat,' he suggested.

'If you like,' she said without enthusiasm. Quite suddenly, she didn't really care where they went or what they did.

He touched her lightly on the arm.

'What's the matter?' he said with a small frown.

'Nothing,' she snapped. At the same time, she jerked her arm away from him. 'And please don't do that,' she added tautly. 'I don't want to be touched.'

His frown deepened, and he looked at her for some time, as if trying to figure out what had brought on this sudden change of mood.

Amy could have explained it to him, but she certainly wasn't going to. There was no way she was going to tell him that the strain of having to spend so much time with him had suddenly started to get to her. He would want to know *why* she found it such a strain to be with him—and she definitely didn't intend to give him an answer to that particular question!

There was a restaurant inside the grounds of the palace, with a fine view of the Bosporus. Amy managed some soup, but only picked at the doner kebab that followed, and couldn't face a dessert at all. Instead, she drank a couple of cups of strong coffee, which only made her already raw nerves feel even more frayed.

She was irrationally annoyed to find that Benedict had eaten everything that he had ordered. The man must have cast-iron nerves. Nothing seemed to get to him.

When they had finished eating, he looked at her. 'What do you want to do now?'

'What do I want to do?' she said edgily. 'I want to go home and get on with my life. I want to be back in my shop, because my mother's absolutely hopeless at running it. She's probably already sold half my stock at less than I paid for it. I want to be somewhere that isn't hot, crowded, crammed with gold and jewels, and exquisitely decorated. I want——' She stopped very abruptly there, because she was suddenly extremely afraid of telling him what else she wanted.

To her relief, Benedict didn't seem to notice that anything was wrong. He didn't even seem to hear the ominous crack in her voice.

'You're just tired,' he said in an unruffled tone. 'You didn't sleep very well last night.'

'How do you know that?' Amy demanded, suddenly alert again. 'Were you watching me?'

'I didn't need to,' he said, still sounding relaxed and even slightly amused. 'You were trying so hard to lie very still and quiet that it was rather obvious that you were awake. People who are asleep move around quite a lot, and their breathing alters.'

'Well, I suppose you'd know all about people's sleeping habits,' she retorted. 'I dare say you've shared your bed plenty of times!'

Benedict gave a small shrug, not even bothering to deny it. 'Does that bother you?' he asked.

'Of course not,' Amy shot back at once, and rather desperately hoped that her voice sounded convincing. 'It's absolutely nothing to do with me.'

'Then why did you bring up the subject?'

It was a perfectly reasonable question, but the problem was that she couldn't produce an equally reasonable answer. So she merely glared at him, pushed away her empty coffee-cup, and then got to her feet.

'I want to go now.'

'Go where?'

'I don't know,' she admitted with a small scowl. 'Just somewhere away from here.'

'We can walk for a while, if you like.'

Amy decided that she was quite willing to go along with that suggestion. She felt very restless again. Perhaps if she kept on the move it would help to get rid of some of the adrenalin that kept building up inside of her.

They made their way back to the old part of Istanbul, and then just wandered round the streets for a couple of hours. By that time, Amy's fascination with the endless shops and the amazing variety of things they had to sell was definitely beginning to pall. The heat, the crowds of people and the non-stop noise began to get to her, and she could feel herself beginning to wilt. It was late afternoon, and she felt as if she had seen more than enough of Istanbul for one day.

Benedict was walking a couple of yards ahead of her. He still looked cool, despite the humidity and the sunshine, and he was showing absolutely no signs of any tiredness.

Amy caught up with him and tugged at his sleeve.

'Can we go back to the hotel now?' Then she shot a rather black look at him, irrationally resenting the fact that he was coping with the strains and exertions of the day so much better than she was. 'Do you even know where the hotel is?'

'Of course,' he replied calmly.

She pulled a face. 'Don't you ever get lost?'

'No. In fact, we're not very far from the hotel. We've been walking in a wide circle.'

Benedict led her through a couple of narrow side-streets, then they emerged into another main thoroughfare. 'The hotel's just down there,' he said, pointing to a side-road just to their left.

Amy gave a sigh of relief. Her legs ached, her head ached, and the rest of her felt positively limp.

'I want a long shower, an hour's sleep and a good meal,' she pronounced.

Benedict's expression changed. 'My guess is that Angeline would like all of those things, as well. But she almost certainly isn't getting them.'

Amy briefly closed her eyes. Angeline, Angeline— didn't he ever stop thinking of her?

Then she immediately felt totally guilty. Her cousin was in very real danger, and probably frightened out of her mind. *She* ought to be thinking of Angeline far more often than she did, instead of whinging about unimportant things like the heat and her own tiredness, or getting wrapped up in her confused feelings for Benedict Kane.

As she trudged into the hotel, she promised herself that Angeline was going to be her top priority from now on. She would do whatever she had to do to get her cousin safely back again.

When they reached their room, she chucked her bag on to the chair and kicked off her sandals.

'Do you mind if I shower first?' she asked.

Before Benedict could answer, though, the telephone suddenly rang.

Amy stopped dead. It was awful, but she didn't want to answer it. She would have given anything to be able to walk out of the door and away from this nightmarish mess.

Instead, however, she forced herself to think of Angeline, and picked up the receiver with a hand that she willed to remain steady.

'Hello,' she said in a quiet tone.

'Who have you got with you?' said the muffled voice of the man who had phoned her before.

'I don't understand——' she began.

'Of course you do!' he cut in roughly. 'You were told to come on your own, but there's a man with you. Who is he?'

Amy began to panic slightly. She put her hand over the receiver and turned to Benedict, her green eyes radiating alarm.

'He knows you're here,' she said rapidly, in a low voice. 'He *was* following us, and he's seen you. He wants to know who you are.'

Benedict looked quite unruffled. 'Tell him that I'm your fiancé,' he instructed.

'*What?*'

'Your fiancé,' he repeated calmly. 'That gives me a perfectly legitimate excuse for being here. You can also tell him that I refused to let you come to Istanbul on your own, but insisted on coming with you.'

Amy swallowed very hard. 'I—I don't think I can say that.'

Benedict's eyes hardened. 'Do it—now!'

She removed her hand from the receiver and cleared her throat.

'The man who's with me, he's—he's——' She gave another nervous cough. 'He's my fiancé,' she finally got out in a rush.

'Why did you bring him with you?' demanded the man at the other end of the phone. 'The letter told you to come on your own.'

'No, it didn't,' Amy said, surprised that she had the nerve to argue with this man who was holding her cousin captive. 'It just told me to book into the Golden Horn hotel. My fiancé wouldn't let me travel all this way and then stay in a strange country by myself. He insisted on coming with me.'

The man growled something under his breath and it didn't sound very polite. He obviously didn't like this new twist in events.

'This means that there might have to be a change of plans,' he muttered at last.

'But you will still let Angeline go?' Amy said with fast-growing anxiety. 'When we've done whatever it is you want us to do, she'll be released and she won't be harmed in any way?'

'I'll get in touch again in a day or two,' said the man in a more decisive tone. 'In the meantime, you and your fiancé had better be very careful not to arouse any suspicions or do anything that's at all stupid.'

'We won't,' Amy said without hesitation. 'I promise that we won't. But why do we have to wait? If you want money, why can't we give it to you straight away?'

He didn't even answer. The phone went dead in her hand, and she slowly replaced the receiver.

'Well?' demanded Benedict tautly. 'Did he buy it? Does he believe I'm your fiancé?'

'I think so,' said Amy. Then her eyes flashed angrily. 'But he didn't like it. He's not even going to get in touch for another couple of days. Coming here with

me was a really bad idea. It could even have put
Angeline's life in danger. Why didn't you stay in
England and let me handle this by myself?'

'Because I thought you might not go through with
it,' he said abruptly. 'Or that you might crack up. I
thought that I needed to be around to hold things
together, and force you to do what was best for
Angeline.'

Amy looked at him rather curiously. 'But you don't
think that way any more?' she said at last.

'You're a lot more capable than I expected. And
I'm beginning to think that you do have some feelings
for your cousin,' he admitted.

'Then why don't you go home, and let me carry on
with this by myself?' she said promptly.

'It's too late for that,' said Benedict. 'The kidnappers will only get suspicious if I suddenly leave.
The two of us are going to have to see this through
to the very end.'

An odd mixture of disappointment and relief rushed
through Amy. Disappointment that there wasn't going
to be a quick end to this nightmarish situation. Relief
that Benedict Kane would be around for at least a few
more days.

In fact, he would be around until Angeline was finally freed. Then he would be gone, and she would
probably never see him again.

Amy was absolutely horrified to find that a small
part of her wished that Angeline could stay a captive
for ever.

CHAPTER FIVE

AMY was totally shocked to discover that her feelings for Benedict were so twisted. For a few moments, she had actually wanted her cousin to stay a prisoner so that she could spend more time with him. That was really sick!

It was a long while before she began to remember everything else that had been said this afternoon. Finally, though, she raised her head and shot a black look at Benedict.

'I don't see why I had to tell that man you were my fiancé,' she said edgily. 'Why couldn't I simply have said you were a friend?'

'Because that would have sounded much more suspicious. Being your fiancé gives me a legitimate excuse for being here, especially if he thinks I'm the possessive and jealous type, who can't stand the thought of you going anywhere on your own.'

Amy gazed at him warily. 'And what's going to make him think you're that type of man?'

Benedict looked back at her. 'We know that we're being watched. We're going to have to make very sure that whoever's watching us gets exactly that impression.'

Her eyes narrowed. 'I don't think I like the sound of that.'

'I don't really care what you like or don't like,' he replied rather tersely. 'As far as I'm concerned, we'll both do whatever has to be done to ensure Angeline's safety. Or was I wrong when I said that part of you really did care what happened to your cousin?'

'No, you weren't wrong,' Amy muttered. At the same time, she remembered the promise she had made to herself just a short while ago. She had vowed that she would do whatever she could to help Angeline. It was just that she hadn't expected that that would include pretending to be Benedict's fiancée! She wasn't at all sure that her frayed nerves were up to that sort of pretence.

'Since they're checking up on us, they probably already know that we're sharing a hotel-room,' went on Benedict. 'That's good, because it adds extra credence to our story.'

'I'm not wearing a ring,' Amy pointed out. 'If they have been watching us, then they must have noticed that.'

'It doesn't really matter. Not all engaged couples bother with a ring, especially if the relationship has already become fairly intimate.'

Amy's throat went uncomfortably dry. 'Intimate?' she repeated cautiously. She didn't even like saying the word. It seemed to imply—oh, she didn't really know *what* it implied. She just knew that it made her feel very funny inside.

Benedict gave a half-smile. 'There's no need to look so nervous. We only have to keep up any kind of pretence when we're out together in public. Here, in this hotel-room, we can just be ourselves.'

That was a lot easier than it sounded, though. Amy was beginning to wonder if she even knew who she really was any more. Certainly not the same girl who had boarded the plane for Istanbul. And she didn't recognise the new, mixed-up and very vulnerable person who had taken her place.

'Why don't you shower and change?' suggested Benedict. 'Then we can go down for dinner.'

'You keep taking everything so calmly,' she said, almost accusingly.

'What's the alternative? It isn't going to help Angeline if we start running around, shouting and panicking.'

'And that's why we're here, isn't it?' she said in a suddenly flat voice. 'To help Angeline. There's no other reason for our being here and doing all of this.'

Benedict shot her a sharp glance, as if he had picked up something from her tone that she hadn't intended to be there.

'Yes,' he said at last, looking at her again through narrowing eyes, 'that's why we're here.'

Amy always became very nervous when that dark gaze drilled into her so intently. She was never sure exactly what he was seeing.

'I think I'll take my shower now,' she blurted out, and scurried into the bathroom.

She hurriedly closed the door behind her, slumped against it and then gave a resigned sigh. She seemed to have spent a lot of the last twenty-four hours locked in this bathroom!

Half an hour later, she had got herself back under some kind of control, and was ready to go down to dinner. Despite everything that had happened, Amy found that she was very hungry. They lingered over their meal for a long time, and she had the impression that Benedict was as reluctant to return to their room as she was.

It was quite late in the evening by the time they finally went back upstairs. The city outside still hummed with noise and movement, but Amy didn't feel part of it in any way. This wasn't a holiday and she wasn't enjoying her stay here. In fact, it was turning out to be just about the most fraught experience of her life!

She went back into the bathroom, cleaned her teeth, wriggled into her baggy nightshirt, and told herself that there wouldn't be any problem getting through the night ahead. She had managed last night without any major catastrophes, hadn't she? Of course, she hadn't slept very much, but she hadn't expected to. She was beginning to wonder if she were ever going to sleep soundly and dreamlessly again!

She returned to the bedroom, hopped straight into bed and pulled the sheet right up to her chin. Benedict was standing with his back to her, looking out of the window. She had the feeling that he had forgotten she was even there, and was sure that he was thinking of Angeline.

'Aren't you going to sleep?' she asked in a rather small voice. It made her feel uncomfortably edgy to see him standing there—tall, powerful in a way that was somehow wholly masculine, and with his thoughts so obviously preoccupied with someone else.

Without saying a word, he left the window and stretched out on the bed, still fully dressed. He clearly didn't intend to sleep—perhaps couldn't sleep. Amy closed her own eyes and prepared herself for a very long night.

Half an hour later, although she hadn't expected to, she suddenly fell into a deep sleep. For a couple of hours she slept soundly, but then she began to have a strange, frightening dream. She was in danger, although she didn't know why or from whom. Someone—or something—was chasing her. She kept running but it got closer and closer, and she *knew* it was going to hurt her when it caught her.

Then it leaped at her—a dark shadow with blazing eyes—and she gave such a loud yell of fear that she woke herself up.

The first thing she saw was the dark shadow, and she shrank back and started to yell again.

A hand clamped itself firmly over her mouth and the shadow spoke to her in a very familiar voice.

'Stop shouting so loudly. Half the hotel staff will be rushing in here in a minute, to see what's going on.'

Amy immediately began to feel extremely embarrassed. 'Sorry,' she mumbled, as the pressure of Benedict's fingers on her mouth lifted. 'I had a bad dream.'

'Do you often have nightmares?'

'Hardly ever.' She couldn't see his face clearly in the darkness, but she was very much aware that he was still sitting on the edge of the bed, which made her nerves feel *extremely* twitchy. 'I'm all right now,' she said quickly. 'You can go back to sleep.'

Benedict didn't move, though. 'What was the nightmare about?'

'I can't remember it very clearly. Something was chasing me. Something dark and dangerous.'

'Mmm,' he said thoughtfully.

Amy didn't like that non-committal response. 'It doesn't really matter what the dream was about,' she said a little irritably. 'Anyway, it's over now. I'm going to try and get some more sleep—if you'll stop talking!'

To her relief, he got the message. He got up and went back to his own bed, and she closed her eyes with some determination. It was over an hour before she drifted back to sleep, though, and she soon started to dream again. There were no more nightmares, but the dreams were disturbing enough to make her toss restlessly. When she finally woke up again, she felt heavy-eyed and listless, as if she hadn't slept at all.

The sun was shining again, with a bright cheerfulness that really grated on her nerves. She would have preferred a dark, overcast day, to match her mood.

Benedict must have woken up earlier than she had, because he had already showered and dressed. Amy crawled under the shower, washed and dried herself, pulled on a pair of jeans and a cotton blouse, and unenthusiastically dragged a comb through the pale blonde tangle of her hair. When she went back out to the bedroom, Benedict was waiting for her.

'Ready for breakfast?' he asked.

'I suppose so.'

His dark gaze fixed on her drawn face. 'What's the matter with you this morning? Or are you feeling bad because of that nightmare you had last night?'

'The dream wasn't important,' she insisted. 'I'm just a bit tired, that's all. And I wish that there was something we could *do* instead of hanging around like this, waiting for phone-calls that never seem to get us any further. When are they going to tell us what we've got to do to get Angeline back again?'

'First of all, they want to make sure that we can be trusted, and that we haven't been to the authorities,' Benedict reminded her. His own mouth was set in a hard line now. 'I don't like this situation any better than you do, but there's virtually nothing we can do about it. We just have to wait until they make their demands.'

'I hate this,' she muttered. Her green eyes flashed. 'And what are we going to do today? Pretend to be tourists again? Walk round looking at the sights, and knowing all the time that we're being watched by the men who've kidnapped Angeline?'

'That's exactly what we're going to do,' Benedict said in a flat tone. 'We obey their instructions to the letter. And we don't do a single thing that will put Angeline in any kind of jeopardy. Now, you'd better come down with me and have something to eat. It's going to be another very long day.'

Amy dearly wished she could tell him that she wasn't going anywhere with him. That wasn't going to help Angeline, though. With a small sigh, she picked up her bag and followed him down to the dining-room.

After they had eaten breakfast, they headed back out into the hot, crowded streets of Istanbul. Amy glanced around nervously.

'Do you suppose they're watching us already?' she muttered to Benedict.

'It's very possible,' he replied. 'So perhaps this would be a good time for you to start acting like my fiancée.'

Amy's green eyes opened wider in alarm. 'What do you mean?'

One of his dark eyebrows gently rose. 'I'm not suggesting anything *too* improper,' he said drily. 'For now, it should be enough to walk along holding hands.'

Amy's palm immediately began to sweat. Surreptitiously, she rubbed it against her trouser leg.

'We didn't hold hands yesterday,' she said edgily.

'No, we didn't,' Benedict agreed. 'Which makes it even more important that we put on a good show today. If we don't touch or look reasonably close to each other, then they're going to get very suspicious. And that's the very last thing that we want to happen.'

Amy's heart had begun to pound in an uncomfortably erratic rhythm. She hadn't been expecting anything quite like this. In fact, she had almost forgotten that she had told the man on the phone that Benedict was her fiancé.

'I really don't think this is necessary——' she began, but then she broke off and gave a huge gulp because Benedict had ignored her protest and slid his hand around hers.

His grip was firm, and his fingers warm and dry. Amy didn't say anything more after that for a long time, because she couldn't. It seemed to be hard even to breathe.

It's ridiculous to feel this way about someone that you don't even know very well, she told herself over and over. Someone who belongs to your cousin, Angeline; who'll go straight back to her as soon as she's free.

They walked on through the streets of Istanbul, and it was alarming how soon she got used to the feel of his hand lightly wrapped around her own. She didn't notice the crowds, the noise, the heat.

Very, very slowly, she came to her senses. This was all make-believe, she reminded herself for the dozenth time, trying to impress that fact on her muddled mind.

You'd better remember that, or you're going to end up in serious trouble.

'Where are we going?' she eventually asked Benedict, making an enormous effort to keep her voice light and normal.

'The church of Haghia Sophia,' he replied. 'And if you're not tired of churches, we'll go on to the Blue Mosque afterwards. It's only a short distance away.'

Amy could already see their minarets rising high up into the sky. Soon the great church of Haghia Sophia was looming up in front of them, with its pale yellow walls and great central dome.

Once they were inside, Benedict let go of her hand, and Amy was alarmed at the disappointment that immediately shot through her. He began to point out the mosaics over the doorways and she looked at them dutifully, although without really seeing them. Then they went on into the central part of the church, and this time she really did catch her breath.

There were rows of great colonnaded arches, and windows which allowed the sun to flood in and illuminate the mosaics. Above all, though, there was the great dome, which seemed to float in the air high above them.

'Very impressive,' Benedict said softly.

'How high is it?' she asked.

He fished the guide-book out of his pocket. 'A hundred and eighty feet. It's also fallen down several times,' he added.

Amy grimaced. 'You might have waited until we were out of here before you told me that!'

'Don't worry,' he said comfortably, 'it's a few hundred years since it last collapsed.'

They walked slowly around the vast interior of the church, and Benedict finally stopped by a column near the entrance. There was a metal cover around the base of the column, with a small hole just big enough to poke a finger through.

'Try touching the column,' he invited.

'Why?' asked Amy suspiciously.

'Just try it.'

A little apprehensively, she stuck her finger through the hole and touched the column itself.

'It feels damp,' she said in surprise.

'It's known as the Sweating Column,' Benedict told her. 'People have been touching it for centuries. They believe it cures eye problems and enables barren women to conceive children.' He gave her a slightly mischievous smile. 'Perhaps I shouldn't have encouraged you to touch it.'

Amy stared back at him, her face suddenly setting into a withdrawn expression. Then she turned round and rapidly walked away from him.

She didn't stop walking until she was back outside in the sunshine. By that time, Benedict had caught up with her. But he didn't say anything. He simply kept pace with her until she finally came to a halt under the shade of a small group of trees.

'Obviously, I said something wrong,' he said at last. 'Are you going to tell me what it is?'

She took a deep breath. 'You didn't say anything wrong,' she replied in a low voice. 'You just reminded me of something that I'd rather forget.'

'Something very personal,' Benedict said with a small frown. He took hold of her hand again and pulled her down on to the grass. Then he settled himself comfortably beside her. 'Do I have to guess what it is?'

'I don't want you to guess,' she said rather sharply. 'I don't even want to talk about it.'

'When people feel like that about something, the one thing that they *should* do is talk about it.'

He had never used quite that tone of voice to her before. Unexpectedly gentle, almost coaxing—it invited confidences.

'I don't think that I can,' she muttered. And certainly not to him.

His dark gaze rested on her assessingly. 'It was just after you touched the Sweating Column. Something that I said upset you.' His eyes narrowed as he thought back. 'Was it when I told you that touching the column was supposed to cure fertility problems? Do *you* have those sort of problems?'

'No,' she said in an almost inaudible voice. 'But it reminded me——'

'Reminded you of what?' he prompted softly.

'It reminded me of a time when I thought I was pregnant,' she blurted out, without looking at him.

A second later, she couldn't believe that she had actually said it. Not to Benedict Kane, the one man whom she *didn't* want to know too much about her.

He was silent for a while, as if waiting to see if she was voluntarily going to tell him anything more. When it became obvious that she wasn't, he shifted his position a little, moving slightly closer. Amy felt a nervous flutter inside of her. Although she didn't know why, she had the feeling that it would be very hard to keep anything from this man if he started asking direct questions.

'How did you feel, when you thought you were pregnant?' he asked at last.

Amy hadn't expected him to ask that. It was a question that wasn't too difficult to answer, though.

'Surprised,' she admitted drily. 'Scared, disbelieving, elated—every half-hour, I used to feel something different!'

'Then you wanted a baby?'

'Not just *a* baby. I didn't try and get pregnant because my maternal instincts were running riot. But when I thought it had happened, I was really starry-eyed for a while. I started dreaming about weddings, being happy ever after, the two of us with the baby——' Her eyes became shadowed. 'I was pretty naïve at the time. Like a school-kid who still believes in fairy-tales with happy endings.'

'When did all this happen?'

'Just over a year ago.'

'You were in love with the father?' he asked, just a little more sharply than seemed necessary.

Amy shrugged. 'At the time, I certainly thought he was very special. I suppose it was because he was the first man I'd had a really serious relationship with.'

Benedict briefly looked sceptical. 'That's hard to believe. You're what—in your early twenties? And you've only had one close relationship?'

'That's because——' Amy began, a little defensively. Then she stopped.

'Because of what?' he prompted.

She gave a soft sigh. She knew that it had been a mistake to get involved in this conversation. She didn't even know how it had happened. A few minutes ago she had resolved not to tell him anything about her private life. And yet here she was, blurting out absolutely everything.

'Because of what?' Benedict asked again. Those dark eyes of his looked at her directly, demanding an answer, and she found it impossible not to give it.

'Because of Angeline,' she mumbled.

His gaze sharpened. 'How does your cousin come into this?'

'Angeline's always been very—competitive, where men are concerned,' she said after a long pause, choosing her words very carefully. 'It's like a game to her. And because I'm her cousin, she seemed to like playing the game even more when I was around.'

Benedict looked as if he didn't much like what he was hearing. Amy couldn't help that, though. After all, *he* was the one who kept asking all the questions.

'Whenever I found anyone I liked, Angeline would try to take him away,' she went on a little wearily. 'I don't think that she meant to be deliberately malicious—or perhaps she did. I've never been quite sure how Angeline's mind works. Anyway, she always succeeded. You've seen both of us, so you know what she's like. She's a little bit more of everything than I am. Prettier, sexier, a better body, more glitz and sparkle——'

'Don't run yourself down like that,' Benedict cut in with unexpected sharpness.

'I'm not.' Amy gave a resigned shrug. 'It's just the way things are. Anyway, when I met Giles, I made sure that I kept him away from Angeline.' She gave a slightly bitter smile. 'I wished afterwards that I hadn't. I'd have been better off if Angeline *had* taken him away from me.'

'He wasn't pleased when you told him you thought you were pregnant?'

Amy's eyes began to flare brightly. 'That's something of an understatement. At first, he kept on trying to insist that it couldn't possibly be his. I told him that it certainly was, and *that* was when he finally told me that he was married! He'd always spent a lot of time away, but I'd thought he was travelling abroad on business trips. That was what he told me, and I was stupid enough to believe him.' She ran her fingers through the pale strands of her hair. 'I was so trusting, so childish. He lied over and over, about absolutely everything, and I didn't once even *consider* that he might be lying. And he wasn't just married. He had four kids! *Four.* And he most certainly didn't want another one, especially if it were mine. He went a little crazy at the thought of my being pregnant. I'd never seen him like that before; he scared me half to death. He kept shouting that there was no way I was going to have that baby—that I'd have to have an abortion. He threatened to drag me to the clinic himself if I wouldn't go voluntarily.'

Benedict's eyes had gone almost black. 'Did he hurt you physically?' he asked tightly.

'He hit me a couple of times,' she admitted in a low voice. 'That really shook me. No one had ever raised a hand to me before.'

He muttered something angrily under his breath. Then he raised his head. 'Bastards like that ought to be locked away.'

'It certainly taught me a few things about men,' she said bitterly. 'And, of course, none of it need have happened. I wasn't pregnant at all; it was just a false alarm. I'm almost glad that it happened, though. At least I managed to get out of the relationship before any serious damage was done.'

'It sounds to me as if he managed to cause quite a lot of damage,' Benedict said grimly.

'In the short-term, things weren't too good,' Amy agreed. 'For a while, I really fell apart. It wasn't just the end of the relationship that got to me, it was all the lies, all the deceit. Then I inherited that money from my uncle, bought the shop, and slowly started to put things back together. And in the long run, perhaps it's been good for me. I'm tougher, not so naïve, I can handle things better.' At least, she had thought she could, until she had met Benedict Kane.

His face was still set into hard lines. 'You shouldn't have to be tough. You're not the type.' He paused, then said in a rather different tone, 'Do you still have any feelings for him?'

'I don't think that I ever did love him—not properly, heart and soul, the way it's meant to be. The whole thing was a very immature sort of affair. Looking back, it's hard to understand how I ever got into it.'

'It's always easy to be wise in retrospect.'

Amy gave him a slightly sharp glance. 'That sounds like the voice of experience talking. Have you done things that *you* regret?'

His dark eyebrows lifted expressively. 'Hasn't everyone?'

She let out a small sigh. 'I suppose so. That's one of the things that helps to make it bearable: knowing that almost everyone makes a real mess of their life at some point.' Then she shot another look at him. 'Do you realise how little I know about you?' she said, with a frown. 'Here I am, telling you things that I always swore I'd never tell anyone, but you're really just a stranger.'

Benedict shrugged. 'It's a well-known fact that it's usually easier to talk to someone that you don't know very well.'

'Well, I think that it's time it worked both ways. How about telling me something about yourself? After all, it looks as if I'm going to have to play the part of your fiancée for at least another couple of days. It might help me to give a more convincing performance if I know more about you.'

'I suppose that makes sense,' he agreed. 'What do you want to know?'

Since she hadn't expected him to fall in with her suggestion so readily, she couldn't think what to ask him. 'Tell me what you do for a living,' she said at last, knowing that it was a rather feeble question, but not quite having the nerve yet to ask anything more personal.

'I thought you knew. I run a handful of companies.'

'A handful?' she repeated, with an expressive grimace. 'Can't you remember *exactly* how many?'

'Seven,' he said with a faint smile.

'What kind of companies?'

'They're mostly connected with the retail trade, particularly fashion. And before you ask, no, I don't design any of the clothes,' he added, his dark eyes briefly gleaming. 'I simply market them as widely and as efficiently as possible.'

'Is it a family business?'

Benedict shook his head. 'I began with one small company that I bought with a windfall inheritance from my grandfather. Then I gradually expanded and bought up other companies as I became more successful.'

'You must have worked very hard.'

'It's easy to do that when you don't have a wife and family making demands on your time.'

'Why *aren't* you married?' Amy asked curiously. Then she flushed slightly as she realised that that was a very personal question to ask.

Benedict looked as if he wasn't going to answer her. A rather dark expression briefly crossed his face, and she guessed that he wasn't used to this sort of inquisition from anyone.

Finally, though, his shoulders lifted in a small shrug. 'It's simply something that's never happened.'

'But why?' she persisted.

He gave a slightly impatient growl. 'Does there have to be a reason?'

'There nearly always is.' Amy's nerve had almost run out, but she couldn't seem to let go of this until she had got an answer. 'Perhaps there was someone you never quite got over?' she suggested hesitantly. 'Someone you wanted, but could never have.'

'No,' Benedict said flatly. His dark eyes fixed on her face. 'And that's why I'm not married. Because I've *never* met anyone like that. I've spent a lot of time in a lot of beds, but they were never the right bed. No woman's ever been the right woman.'

Amy swallowed rather hard. 'I see,' she said, almost in a whisper. 'But you said—you thought that Angeline——' But she couldn't finish the sentence. For some reason, the thought of Angeline being the right woman for Benedict Kane was almost unbearable.

'When I met Angeline, I thought that perhaps——' He abruptly stopped for a few moments, looked as if he didn't intend to say anything more, but then added in an even brusquer tone, 'I don't know, we didn't have enough time. Perhaps when she's free——'

They both fell silent as they remembered the reason why they were here, in Istanbul.

Amy was the first one to break the silence. 'Do your family know you're here?' she asked in a subdued voice. 'Do they know about your—involvement with my cousin?'

Benedict shook his head. 'I like to keep my personal life private. I did ring my parents and tell them I'd be away for a few days, on a business trip. I travel abroad quite often, so they didn't have any reason to question it. There didn't seem any point in worrying them unnecessarily by telling them I might be involved in a possible kidnapping.'

'Don't you have any brothers or sisters you can confide in?'

'I had an older brother,' he said, after a short pause. 'He was killed in a smash-up on the motorway. He didn't cause the accident, but he was the one who died.'

'That's a dreadful thing to happen,' Amy said softly.

'Yes,' he said, in flat agreement. Then he made a rather obvious effort to push it out of his mind, as if it were something that he couldn't bear to think about for very long. 'This conversation is becoming distinctly morbid,' he said, getting quickly to his feet. 'If one of the kidnappers is watching us, they're going to get very suspicious if we sit around with gloomy faces, looking more and more depressed. We're meant to be engaged, remember? They'll expect us to be worried about Angeline, but they'll also expect us to look moderately happy when we're together. Engaged couples are meant to enjoy each other's company.'

'I don't think I'm very good at being a fiancée—even a temporary one,' Amy said, with a grimace. 'Can't we just drop this pretence?'

'And tell the kidnappers what? That we lied? That isn't going to help Angeline. The kidnappers have to *trust* us, they've got to believe that we're following their instructions and that we're exactly who we told them we are. So let's start putting some realism into the performance, or they're going to guess the truth.'

He gripped hold of Amy's hand and hauled her to her feet. Instead of letting go of her, though, he pulled her even closer and then slid his hands around her waist, his fingers holding her so firmly that there was no chance to pull away.

'What are you *doing*?' she yelped in alarm.

'Stop squealing and start acting,' he instructed roughly. 'Engaged couples like to kiss, and that's exactly what we're going to do.'

'We are not——' she began indignantly, then her protest was cut off by the hard pressure of his mouth.

She supposed that he was kissing her so hard because he wanted to shut her up. Or perhaps he always kissed like this. Or maybe he was simply getting his own back for all the times when she had irritated him.

Finally, he had to release that pressure just a fraction in order to breathe.

Amy dragged a shuddering breath into her own constricted lungs; then she glared up at him.

'Stop it!' she hissed at him.

'Not yet,' Benedict said implacably. 'If you don't like it—and it's fairly obvious that you don't,' he added in a hard tone, 'then close your eyes and remember that you're doing this for Angeline.'

Amy had already closed her eyes, though, because she needed to blot out the sight of his face so close to hers. And he had got it wrong about her not liking it. She liked it far too much! That was the reason why she was panicking inside. If he realised just how *much* she liked it, then all the advantages were going to be on his side in the future, and that was something she didn't want—couldn't allow—to happen.

Another kiss followed, and a deep shudder ran right through her, seeming to penetrate right to the very depths of her soul. His mouth was warm and dry; his tongue didn't explore but she suddenly had the feeling that it wanted to.

The sun burned down all around them, but didn't touch them as they stood under the shade of the tree. All the same, Amy felt scorched inside. This second kiss was killing her, and she didn't even understand why.

When Benedict finally let go of her, it was hard to stand up unsupported. His dark eyes looked down at her, almost black and quite unreadable.

'I think that's enough pretence for one day,' he said in an unexpectedly terse voice.

Amy didn't answer him; couldn't answer him. Benedict turned round and strode off, and she stumbled along after him, feeling as if everything in her life had just changed forever.

It was only a kiss, she told herself over and over, quite frantically. People kissed every day.

But they didn't feel like this afterwards. They wouldn't be willing to give half of their life for just one more kiss exactly like it.

You're going crazy! Amy muttered to herself in bewilderment. The sun, the heat, the strange, exotic surroundings—they're all getting to you.

But she knew she was wrong. None of those things were responsible for the way she felt. It was Benedict Kane who was getting to her.

And that was the craziest thing of all!

CHAPTER SIX

AMY seemed to go through the rest of the day in a state of shock. She talked to Benedict, ate lunch, walked and moved in an apparently normal manner, but part of her didn't seem to be there at all. The feeling of unreality was actually quite pleasant. It seemed to separate her from what had happened earlier.

In the afternoon, they visited the Blue Mosque. She dutifully stared at the six slender, elegant minarets that flanked it, the two hundred and sixty windows that admitted a flood of light, the exquisitely patterned tiles that covered the walls, the pillars and the dome— most of them coloured blue and giving the mosque its name.

When they finally left, it was time to return to the hotel. Despite the sense of unreality that still had her in its grip, Amy's heart began to thump faster at the prospect of spending another night sharing a room with Benedict. The prospect frightened her half to death, and yet gave her a curious kind of pleasure. And all the time there was a strong undertone of guilt because she knew that she shouldn't be thinking any of these things; she should be totally preoccupied with Angeline, and concentrating only on getting her cousin free again.

As she and Benedict entered the hotel-room, the phone began to ring. Amy's heart began to pound for a very different reason. With an awkward, jerky movement, she snatched hold of the receiver.

'Yes?' she said edgily.

'Be at the Galata Tower tomorrow morning at eleven o'clock,' said the man's voice at the other end. Then he severed the connection.

'Hello?' she said, jiggling the phone a little frantically. 'Please, don't go! I want to ask you——'

It was too late. There was no one at the other end.

'He wants us to be at the Galata Tower tomorrow, at eleven,' she repeated to Benedict dully.

'That isn't too far from here,' he said. 'It's just on the other side of the Golden Horn. We can cross at the Galata Bridge, and from there it's just a few minutes' walk.'

'But we still aren't getting anywhere!' she burst out in frustration. 'He hasn't even told us if Angeline is alive and well. *Anything* could have happened to her since they snatched her!'

'Angeline is fine,' Benedict said at once. 'It wouldn't make sense for them to harm her—not if they want us to pay for her safe return.'

'Don't treat me like a child,' Amy shot back angrily. All her nerve-ends were suddenly and vividly alive again. The comforting sense of unreality had gone, and she had the feeling that it wouldn't come back again. 'Kidnappings are always dangerous. And the victims *aren't* always returned safely. Don't pretend that they are!'

Benedict gripped her arms and shook her lightly, his own features changing and setting into a shadowed mask. 'Yes, there are risks,' he agreed tightly. 'But we can minimise those risks by using our heads, behaving sensibly, and following the kidnappers' instructions as closely as we can.'

'We're giving in to them,' she muttered. 'I hate that!'

His eyes suddenly blazed. 'And you think that I don't? But our own feelings don't matter right now. Getting Angeline back is the only thing that's important.'

He seemed to realise that he was still holding on to her, and he abruptly let go, then turned away from her. Amy stared at him with dull eyes. He obviously didn't want to touch her or even be near her. She didn't have to worry about sharing this room with him. There wouldn't be any more kisses while they were alone here together. There didn't *need* to be any kisses. That had been just a performance that had to be put on in case any of the kidnappers were watching.

With a jolt of shock, Amy realised that she was almost beginning to hate her cousin, because she was the only one that Benedict thought about. Everything he did was because of her. She was totally ashamed of feeling like that, but at the same time, she couldn't seem to stop.

It ruined her appetite, and when they went down to dinner she could only pick at the pieces of tender lamb that had been rolled in flour, sautéd in butter, and then served in a broth of fresh vegetables, herbs and spices. For dessert, there were wafer-thin layers of sweet pastry stuffed with walnut, but Amy only managed to force down one mouthful, and then pushed the plate away.

Benedict frowned at her. 'It isn't going to help if you stop eating.'

'As far as I can see, nothing's going to help,' she said in a defeated tone.

'What do you mean by that?'

Suddenly scared that she might give something away, even by just looking at him, she looked down at her plate and the remains of her uneaten meal.

'Nothing,' she said in a low voice. 'I'm tired, that's all. I need some sleep.'

'We both need some sleep,' he said rather shortly.

Amy glanced up at him, and saw that he was right. There were dark shadows of tiredness under his eyes, and she remembered that she had woken him last night, when she had had that nightmare.

'I suppose that's my fault,' she muttered. 'I disturbed you when I had that bad dream.'

'None of this is anyone's fault,' Benedict said, in the same terse voice. He got to his feet. 'Let's go back upstairs and get to bed. Tomorrow's going to be a difficult day and it isn't going to help Angeline if we're asleep on our feet.'

Half an hour later, she was lying on her bed, staring into the darkness. Outside, the city was as noisy as usual, but it wasn't the mingled sound of voices and music and traffic that was keeping her awake.

With a carefully suppressed sigh, Amy turned over and resolutely closed her eyes. She remembered, rather enviously, all those nights when she had simply clambered into bed and gone straight to sleep. Now she was beginning to wonder if she were ever going to sleep properly again.

A long way into the night, though, her breathing slowed and became more even, her body relaxed, and she finally drifted off into the welcoming darkness.

The stretch of deep, peaceful sleep didn't last for long, however. Soon she started dreaming again, muddled and confused dreams at first, but then they became more vivid—more frightening. Then the same nightmare that she had had last night began all over again.

The dark shape, never clearly seen, started chasing her. Amy didn't know why she was so scared of it, she just knew that she had to get away. No matter how fast she ran, though, she couldn't escape from it. It stalked her; played with her. She ran faster still, heart pounding and legs shaking. And then, just when she thought she had finally got away, it loomed up in front of her and *pounced* on her...

Amy let out a loud yell of pure fear, and woke herself up.

She also woke up Benedict. He switched on the small lamp beside the bed, came over and frowned down at her.

'Another bad dream?'

'Yes,' she muttered. Then, seeing the look of disapproval on his face, she added defensively, 'I can't *help* having them. I know it's inconvenient and I keep waking you up, but there's really not much I can do about it.'

'What was this one about?'

'It was the same as the last one. Something dark and dangerous was chasing me.'

One of Benedict's eyebrows gently rose. 'It sounds rather Freudian to me.'

'And what exactly is that supposed to mean?' she snapped at him, tiredness and tension fraying her nerves.

He shrugged. 'I'm no expert, but it's fairly common knowledge that that kind of dream is often caused by some sexual hang-up. The 'dark and dangerous' thing that's frightening you is the darker, wilder side of your own nature. If you suppress it when you're awake, or simply refuse to admit that it exists, it pops up and haunts you in your dreams.'

'Thanks for the lecture,' Amy said coldly. 'I don't believe a word of it, but you obviously feel better now that you've found a rational explanation for my nightmare.'

'It doesn't really matter whether or not I feel better about it,' Benedict pointed out. 'You're the one who's having the bad dreams. And my guess is that you're going to keep on having them if you won't try and sort out the underlying problem that's causing them.'

'I don't have any problems!' Amy retorted furiously. 'At least, I didn't until *you* came into my life.'

She stopped there very abruptly, realising what she had just said. Panic replaced the swift surge of temper. Perhaps he didn't hear what I said, she prayed silently. And if he did, please, *please* God, don't let him understand it.

Benedict's dark gaze was resting on her assessingly, and Amy waited tensely for him to say something. She didn't breathe, didn't blink, didn't move a single muscle.

In the end, though, he looked away again without saying anything. Then he got up and walked slowly over to the window.

Amy let out the pent-up breath she had been holding. But she was careful to do it very quietly. One thing she was absolutely determined about: she wasn't going to make any more slip-ups like that!

She slid off the bed, went into the bathroom, and splashed cold water over the flushed skin of her face. When she returned to the bedroom, Benedict was still standing by the window. As she came in, he turned to confront her, and the expression on his face was different from any she had seen there before.

'I've decided that there really isn't any reason for us to go on sharing a room,' he said without preamble. 'I think it would be better if we booked a separate room for you tomorrow.'

'Because I keep disturbing your sleep?' Amy said stiffly.

'You're certainly beginning to disturb me,' Benedict replied in an unexpectedly soft voice.

She stared at him. 'What do you mean by that?'

'Nothing that you need to worry about. It's just that this is the first time in my life that I've shared a room with a woman without sleeping with her. At first, it was something of a novelty. But the novelty seems to be wearing off.'

'You're sick of having me around?' Amy tried to control the sudden wobble in her voice, and was relieved that she seemed to have succeeded.

'Not exactly. But having you around at night could become a problem, if it goes on for very much longer.'

His face had become quite unreadable, now. And it was impossible to tell anything from his tone of voice.

All the same, Amy's instincts clearly told her that it would be a good idea to put an immediate stop to this conversation. Instead, though, she found herself asking him another question.

'What sort of problem?'

'The usual kind,' he replied rather drily. 'I'm not used to living like a monk, but just recently I've been *very* celibate. It isn't something that I think I can keep up for much longer.'

Amy forced her suddenly constricted throat to work. 'You'll be all right once you've got Angeline back again,' she forced herself to say.

Benedict gave an odd smile. 'Believe it or not, I haven't slept with your cousin.'

'You haven't?' The two words came out as an enormous gasp of surprise and relief. Realising how they must have sounded, she struggled hard to recover herself, although she didn't altogether manage it. 'But—why?' she couldn't stop herself from saying. Then she went bright red. 'Sorry,' she mumbled. 'I've no right to ask that question.'

'I don't mind answering it,' he said, to her astonishment. 'The reason I didn't sleep with Angeline was because I didn't want to jump straight into a physical relationship with her. There were other things I wanted to know about her first—things which I thought might be more important.'

'And were they?' she asked, her throat almost closing up completely as she waited tensely for his reply.

'For a while, it seemed that they might be. Now, though, I'm not so sure.'

'Why?'

'I don't think I want to answer that question right now.' He shifted position slightly restlessly, as if he were suddenly finding this conversation uncomfortable. 'But I do think it would be a good idea if you booked into another room tomorrow.'

'Because you want to sleep with *me*?' Amy blurted out. An instant later, she just couldn't believe that she had asked that question. How completely humiliating and embarrassing if he said no. And what on earth would she do if he said yes...?

But Benedict simply gave another rather strange smile. 'I think that's one more question that would be better left unanswered for now,' he said.

Amy couldn't leave it alone, though. It was like obsessively picking at a painful wound, knowing that it was going to make it worse, but quite unable to stop doing it.

'It's because I *look* like Angeline, isn't it?' she said in a suddenly dull tone. 'We wouldn't be having this problem if I had dark hair, and was short or fat. I've become a sort of substitute for her. Something you'd like to play around with until you can get the real thing back again.'

At that, Benedict's face altered and he took half a dozen steps towards her.

'I don't play around with women. Not unless they *want* to be played with. Mutual fun and pleasure is fine. But I'm not interested in any other kind of games. And I was wrong when I told you that you looked like Angeline. You're not like her at all.'

'Yes, I am,' Amy insisted. 'Our eyes are a different colour, that's all.'

'Your hair is different,' Benedict corrected her. 'Paler, silkier, longer. Your face is more delicate, your eyes larger, your mouth softer. You're not quite so tall, not quite so thin. You walk more lightly, move more gracefully. You argue a lot more than she does, but your voice is less harsh——' He stopped there fairly abruptly, as if he had never meant to say all of that.

Amy stared at him in astonishment. 'You've noticed all those things about me?'

'It wasn't too difficult,' he said, a dry note returning to his voice. 'We've hardly spent any time apart for the last couple of days.'

She was rather nervously biting her bottom lip, nevertheless. Where was all this leading? Not to any place where she wanted to go, she was sure of that! And certainly not to any place where it was at all *wise* to go. Amy forced herself to remember that men often said things they didn't mean in the dark hours of the night. Why should Benedict Kane be any different? He had suddenly realised that he wanted something— sex, fun, physical relief? Amy wasn't sure what it was. But, like all men, he would try to get it, if he could. And in the morning, all those soft words would be deliberately and conveniently forgotten.

Her only advantage was that he didn't know yet how vulnerable she was. He had no idea that her own nerves and emotions had been in a complete turmoil ever since they had arrived in Istanbul. And she had to make very sure that he never found out!

'Perhaps we could get that separate room right now,' she said bluntly.

Benedict glanced at his watch. 'At three in the morning? I don't thing they'd appreciate it if we went down and demanded to change rooms!' His dark eyes studied her. 'Why are you so anxious to run away? Is it because of what I've said to you tonight?'

'Of course not,' Amy denied vehemently. 'Anyway, it was *you* who suggested that I should get another room.'

The corners of his mouth gave a slight twitch. 'I'm beginning to think that wasn't one of my better suggestions.'

'I think it's very sensible,' she said firmly. 'We don't need to share a room any more.'

His tone changed yet again. 'Perhaps I need to,' he said, and his voice had taken on an almost velvet texture.

Amy looked at him warily. 'What do you mean by that?'

He didn't answer her directly. 'Do you remember when I kissed you today?' he asked instead.

She certainly did! She wasn't going to let him think those couple of kisses had been anything special, though. 'That was just play-acting,' she reminded him. 'A display that we put on for the benefit of the kidnappers, in case they were watching us.'

'It was the nicest piece of play-acting that I can remember,' Benedict said softly.

'Well, it meant nothing to me!' she retorted curtly. 'I'd forgotten all about it until you mentioned it.'

'Then let me remind you how it went,' he murmured.

His movements were as silky-smooth as his voice. And deceptively fast. His arms coiled round her, the warmth of his mouth closed over hers, and she didn't even remember seeing him move. Sheer panic began to gather inside Amy as she realised that this kiss was *exactly* like the one he had given her this afternoon. It seemed to touch all the dark, secret corners of her soul, and if just a kiss could do that, then what on earth would happen if she let it go any further?

A little frantically, she began to wriggle in his arms, trying desperately to break free. He released her mouth for a moment, and his eyes, almost black now, suddenly blazed down at her.

'Stop that,' he ordered.

To her amazement—and disbelief—she immediately obeyed. Benedict muttered something in satisfaction, and then returned his attention to her mouth.

This kiss was different, more intense, as if he had suddenly discovered that he wanted even more than he had thought. His tongue gently licked, as if he liked the taste of her, and his hands began to inch their way more intimately around her body.

Amy was terrified by this new attack. She might just have been able to cope with a kiss. Anything more and she was drifting straight into the realms of pure danger.

He doesn't want *you*, she reminded herself over and over with grim forcefulness. He's missing Angeline; and there hasn't been a woman in his bed for far too long. You're here, and he's hoping you're available. And if he goes on like this for much longer, you will be available, she told herself with a fresh rush of horror, as she realised that his fingers were exploring now with new intent. You've got to put a stop to this. Find some way of making him let go of you.

But Benedict clearly didn't want to let go. One thumb lightly brushed the underswell of her breast, and although Amy gritted her teeth and swore to herself that she wasn't going to show the slightest flicker of response, he must have detected some faint reaction because he gave a small grunt of pleasure. Then his palm smoothly followed in the wake of his thumb, sliding over the soft, full flesh and provoking such a devastating trail of reaction in Amy that she very nearly gave up completely at that point. How

could she possibly fight any of this? For the last couple
of days, she had felt that he could pole-axe her with
just a look. And right now, he was doing a lot more
than looking!

Benedict briefly released her mouth. 'Do you want
to know something strange?' he said musingly.

Amy wasn't at all sure that she did. Enough strange
things had been happening lately. She didn't feel that
she could cope with even one more.

But he carried on speaking without waiting for her
answer. 'When I kissed you this afternoon outside the
Blue Mosque, for the first time in a very long time,
I stopped thinking about Angeline. For those few
minutes, it was as if she didn't even exist.'

'But she does exist,' Amy reminded him in a taut,
strained voice. 'She's been kidnapped, she's probably
terrified, and she's relying on us to get her free. And
we're not going to do that by behaving like this!'

'All right,' he said, his own voice sounding remarkably relaxed. 'First, we get Angeline released.
And then we deal with this.'

'There isn't anything to deal with,' Amy insisted,
stubbornly ignoring the fast, uneven beat of her
pulses, that was telling her something very different.

His dark gaze locked on to hers challengingly, but
she refused to be browbeaten into admitting that she
had lied. If she ever gave in and admitted how easily
he could get to her, how even a couple of kisses could
leave her nerves feeling totally shredded, then she
would be finished.

'I think that it's time we started thinking of Angeline
and nothing else,' she said, staring straight back at
him. 'It's totally selfish to get side-tracked by something like this, when she's still in such danger.'

But Benedict refused to give up so easily. 'And what exactly *is* it that's side-tracking us?'

'Nothing of any importance,' Amy shot back at once, hoping desperately that she was lying convincingly.

He didn't look as if he had believed a single word she had said. To her utter relief, though, he began to move away from her, walking slowly back to the far side of the room.

'Perhaps you're right,' he said in a low, thoughtful tone, almost as if he were talking to himself. 'Maybe this isn't a good time or the right place. We do seem to be getting our priorities rather mixed up.'

Amy scurried back into bed and pulled the sheet tightly around her. 'I'm going to get a couple more hours of sleep,' she said in what she hoped was a very firm voice. 'And I think you'd better do the same. We're going to need all our wits about us when we keep that appointment at the Galata Tower.'

This time, Benedict didn't answer her. Instead, he stared out of the window for a few minutes. Then he walked back to his own bed, stretched out and appeared to go to sleep.

Amy didn't sleep, of course. She hadn't expected to. Her heart was still thumping erratically, and she couldn't forget, even for a second, how she had felt when Benedict's hands had begun to roam over her, casually exploring.

Except that *that* was the trouble. For him, it *had* just been a casual encounter. He had no idea that every time he came near her every single inch of her skin began to prickle in a primitive and uncontrollable response.

The last couple of hours of the night crawled by, and the room at last began to lighten as the sun finally drifted back up into the sky. Both of them got up early, but they didn't say a word to each other as they showered and dressed.

It was Benedict who finally broke the silence. He glanced at his watch, and then at her.

'We might as well go down for breakfast. We've plenty of time. It won't take us long to walk to the Galata Tower.'

'I don't think I feel very hungry,' Amy said in a low voice.

A light frown crossed his face. 'You're not sulking because of last night, are you?'

That made her head shoot up. *'Sulking?'* she repeated, her green eyes briefly flaring.

'Come to think of it, you've been behaving rather oddly for the last couple of days,' said Benedict, his frown deepening.

'I certainly have not,' she denied at once. 'And I'm *not* sulking. I never sulk.'

'Then why aren't you talking to me?'

'You haven't said a word this morning, either,' Amy reminded him.

'I got the impression that you didn't want me to.'

'There are a lot of things that I don't want you to do,' she snapped edgily. 'But that doesn't usually seem to stop you!'

He looked at her thoughtfully. 'We're talking about something else now, aren't we?'

'Are we?' she retaliated in the same edgy tone. 'You tell me.'

'I don't think I can,' he said after a short pause. 'I'm not sure that I understand what's going on here.'

Amy's stomach gave a nervous flip. She didn't *want* him to understand! And she didn't want this conversation to go any further.

'I think we should go down to breakfast,' she said shortly. 'We'll have to leave soon, for the Galata Tower.'

'Are you trying to change the subject?'

'I'm trying to tell you that you seem to have stopped thinking about Angeline, stopped worrying about her. All you seem to want to talk about is us, and we're not important.'

Benedict's eyes began to darken. 'I'm as concerned about Angeline's safety as you are.'

'Then show it,' she challenged him. 'When we first met, *you* kept accusing *me* of not caring. It seems to be the other way round now. But I suppose that's typical of men,' she added with deliberate scorn. 'They begin to get a little frustrated, and they can't think of anything else except doing something about that frustration.'

As soon as she saw the rigid set of Benedict's face, Amy regretted that she had ever opened her mouth. This was definitely the wrong time to say that kind of thing!

He took a couple of steps forward and, when he spoke, his voice had a very dangerous undertone.

'Are you saying that, as far as I'm concerned, Angeline can go to hell? That all I can think about right now is finding someone to take to bed?'

Amy stood up to him sturdily. 'I'm saying that you certainly don't seem to be giving Angeline your full attention any more.'

For just an instant, Benedict looked angry enough to hit her. Amy actually flinched slightly, even though his hands stayed locked by his sides.

His almost violent reaction seemed to shake him. He made a visible effort to control himself. Then he swung round, and strode quickly over to the far side of the room.

'This whole thing is getting ridiculous and quite out of hand,' he said tersely at last, swinging back round to face her. 'I don't think it's any good for us to go on like this. And it certainly isn't helping Angeline.'

'What do you suggest we do about it?' She was amazed that her own voice sounded so steady. Inside, she felt just about ready to fall apart!

'The obvious solution is for you to go back to England. I'll stay here and deal with the kidnappers' demands.'

'No!' she said at once. 'There's no way I'm going to do that.'

'Don't you trust me to negotiate Angeline's release?'

'So far, you've done absolutely nothing to make me believe that I *can* trust you.'

His almost black gaze locked on to her over-bright eyes. Amy forced herself to stare straight back at him, even though her stomach was positively churning now.

'What do I have to do to convince you?' he challenged her. His dark eyes glittered. 'Promise that I'll never lay another finger on you?'

'That would certainly help.'

'And what if I don't want to make a promise like that?' he said more softly.

'I don't see why you shouldn't,' Amy got out in a distinctly strangled tone. 'I don't mean anything to you. And you don't feel anything for me—except, perhaps, annoyance when I argue with you and make you angry. It ought to be easy to make a promise like that.'

Benedict kept looking at her for a very long time. Amy began to feel as if she would soon melt away completely under the intensity of that dark gaze.

Finally, though, his eyes moved away from her. 'Yes, it should be easy to make that kind of promise,' he said in a flat tone. Then he began to move towards the door.

'Where are you going?' asked Amy.

'Down to Reception, to book you into a separate room.' For just an instant, his eyes swung back to her. 'That is what you want, isn't it?'

'Yes, it's what I want,' she mumbled, and was amazed at how hard it was to get those few words out.

Benedict left the room, slamming the door with unnecessary force behind him, and Amy sank down weakly into the nearest chair.

What was happening? she wondered in confusion. What was going on between them? She understood why *she* was having problems coping with this constant closeness to Benedict, but it didn't make any sense that he should suddenly become so uptight.

Poor Angeline, she thought with a wave of compassion and guilt. *She* was the one they should be thinking and worrying about, and yet she was somehow getting pushed into the background. That wasn't right, and it had to stop.

Perhaps everything would finally be settled after they had been to the Galata Tower and met the kidnappers. Then they could all go back home, and get on with their normal lives.

Only Amy wasn't at all sure that her life was ever going to be completely normal again.

CHAPTER SEVEN

AFTER a fairly unsuccessful attempt to choke down some breakfast, Amy set off for the Galata Tower with Benedict.

As always, Benedict seemed to know exactly where he was going. That was the one advantage that Amy could think of—in fact, the *only* advantage—in having him around. She would have been absolutely useless at finding her own way around Istanbul. She would probably have got lost every time she set foot outside the hotel.

They had to cross the Golden Horn at the Galata Bridge. Amy had thought that the streets of Istanbul were crowded, but the crowds milling around the ends of the bridge seemed to set new records! There were street merchants on every square inch of space, selling everything from birdsong whistles, to plastic helicopters on sticks. Fruit and vegetable stalls made a bright display, shoe-shine boys touted for customers, and other younger boys toted around ancient-looking bathroom-scales, trying to persuade people to weigh themselves for a very modest fee.

The boats tied up all around the bridge only added to the congestion. On some of them, fish was being fried. Then it was shoved between a thick wedge of fresh, crusty bread, and sold to hungry passers-by. Ferries trundled past, on their way up and down the Bosporus, while larger cruise ships sailed by more sedately.

Benedict hadn't spoken since leaving the hotel, and Amy didn't try to break the silence. In fact, she didn't even know if she could make herself heard above the loud chatter of voices, the shouts of the street vendors, and the general confusion.

They joined the steady stream of people crossing to bridge. A lot were obviously tourists, but there were also porters bent nearly double under enormous loads; shrouded women obediently walking three feet behind their husbands; a group of gypsies with dark, flashing eyes and strong, aggressive faces; and even businessmen rushing across, clutching their briefcases.

When they were halfway across, Benedict suddenly stopped. 'This is probably one of the best views in Istanbul,' he said, looking out across the Bosporus.

Amy stared at him in amazement. 'We're not here to admire the views!' she reminded him in a sharp voice.

'We've plenty of time. We don't have to be at the Galata Tower for almost another hour.'

'I'd sooner arrive early than get there too late because we stopped to admire the scenery,' she said tartly.

'Then let's keep moving,' he replied in a flat tone.

He walked off fairly quickly. Despite everything she had said, Amy found her gaze involuntarily drifting over the views all around them before she followed him. He was right, they *were* impressive. She could see the walls of the Topkapi Palace, the great domes and minarets of the mosques, and the huddled buildings all around them, all massing together in an utterly distinctive skyline. Then there was the river itself, full of movement and life and colour, with boats of all shapes and sizes either churning busily through the water, or moored peacefully along the banks.

Then she realised that Benedict was some way ahead of her, and she hurried to catch up with him before she lost him completely in the crowd.

As they neared the far side of the bridge, Benedict pointed ahead of them.

'That's the Galata Tower,' he said briefly.

Amy stared in the direction in which he was pointing, and saw the Tower rising up from the mass of buildings all around it, looking like a rather fat and dumpy space rocket. Despite the heat, she gave a small shiver. One of Angeline's kidnappers was waiting for them there. Perhaps they were finally going to find out what had happened to her cousin, and how they could get her safely back again.

The narrow, winding streets leading to the tower were congested, but the crowds seemed miraculously to part before Benedict, letting him through. Amy trotted along in his wake, wishing that today were already over. It was a wish that she seemed to have made every day since she had been in Istanbul, but it had never been granted! In fact, the days just seemed to be getting longer and longer. There were times when she thought they would *never* end.

When they reached the Tower, Benedict paid the entrance fee, and they went inside.

'Where do we go now?' Amy asked.

'To the top, I suppose. There's a viewing-platform up there. That seems the obvious place for a rendezvous of this kind.'

The lift took them up to the seventh floor, then they walked up a couple of flights of stairs, and out on to the viewing-platform.

There were a lot of people already up there, but Amy didn't notice them straight away. The view from the top was too spectacular, with Istanbul and the Bosporus spread out beneath them.

Benedict looked at her and then gently raised one dark eyebrow. 'Weren't you the one who said that this wasn't the time to admire the scenery?' he reminded her.

Her green gaze swivelled away from the fascinating, exotic scene below. 'Then what *are* we meant to do?' she asked edgily.

'I've no idea,' he admitted. 'Wait here, I suppose, and hope someone contacts us.'

'Can't you come up with a more positive suggestion than that?' she said rather scathingly.

When he answered, his own tone was much sharper. 'If I could think of one single thing we could do to help Angeline, then I'd do it.'

'I know,' she muttered. 'Sorry; I just feel jumpy. I hate all this hanging around, not being able to do anything, and all the time feeling so—so——'

'Impotent?' he offered, when she couldn't find quite the right word.

Amy gave a faint, wry smile. 'That wasn't quite the word I was going to use. And I shouldn't think that's something that *you* ever feel!'

His own mouth curled into a very brief smile. 'Up until now, it's never been a problem,' he agreed. Then he looked around and frowned, the brief lightening of his mood already over. 'How long do they expect us to wait here?'

'It's only just eleven o'clock,' Amy pointed out. More people were coming out on to the viewing-platform, and she eyed them nervously. Any one of them could be one of the kidnappers. None of them came anywhere near them, though. They went straight over to admire the views and take photographs.

They stayed at the top of the Tower for over an hour. At one point, the platform became really crowded, with people jostling past them and almost pushing them aside in their eagerness to gaze at the view. Then the congestion eased off a little as it drew nearer to lunchtime, and many of the sightseers went off in search of something to eat.

'No one's going to come, are they?' Amy said at last, with a despondent sigh. 'They're just playing games with us. Perhaps they don't intend to let Angeline go at all,' she added, a note of panic entering her voice as she realised just what that would mean to her cousin.

'I'm beginning to think that someone could certainly be playing games with us,' Benedict agreed in an unexpectedly grim voice. 'But on the other hand, perhaps this was simply some kind of test. They might have been checking that we were willing to turn up at the right place at the right time. Once they're satisfied they can trust us, they'll set up a genuine meeting.'

'What do we do now?' she asked in a forlorn voice.

'Go back to the hotel, I suppose, and wait for them to make contact again.' Then Benedict looked at her rather sharply. 'You're not crying, are you?'

'Of course not,' she said fiercely. 'My eyes are watering a little, that's all. It's probably the bright sunshine. I'll put on my sunglasses.'

She fumbled around in her bag for the glasses. Instead, though, she found a folded sheet of paper that she certainly hadn't put there.

Slowly, she brought it out and stared at it. 'This isn't mine,' she said rather shakily. 'Someone must have slipped it into my bag.'

Benedict took it from her, opened it out, and let his dark gaze skim over it.

'What does it say?'

'They want five thousand pounds, as a down-payment,' Benedict replied in a grim voice. 'We're to leave it under the bench in the north corner of the gardens of the Topkapi Palace, wrapped in an old newspaper.'

Amy swallowed. 'When do we have to deliver it?'

'Tomorrow morning, at eleven o'clock.'

'And when we've given them the money, how long will it be before they free Angeline?'

'They're not going to free her yet. This is simply a down-payment,' Benedict reminded her. 'They want a sign of good faith from us—an assurance that we're willing to pay whatever they demand in return for Angeline's safe return.'

'Then they're going to be disappointed. I don't even have five thousand, let alone the big sum that they're obviously going to ask for before they finally let Angeline go.'

'How much *can* you raise?' Benedict asked her.

'No more than a couple of thousand. I've already told you, I can't touch the investments my uncle left me. And even if I could somehow convince the trustees of the estate that this is a real emergency, and they agreed to let me sell the shares, it would probably take *weeks* before all the legal formalities were completed and I could actually get my hands on the cash. And I don't think the kidnappers would be willing to wait that long,' she finished rather despairingly.

'No, I don't think that they would,' he agreed. 'So you'd better let me pay the ransom demands.'

'Can you afford to do that?'

'If I couldn't, I wouldn't have offered,' Benedict replied drily.

'No, I suppose not,' she muttered. Then her mouth set into a more determined line. 'But I can't let you pay. Angeline's my cousin, and my problem. I'll somehow find a way to raise the money.'

'How?' he asked calmly.

'I don't know!' Then, with an effort, she got control of herself again. 'I'll probably be able to borrow it. I can use my uncle's investments as collateral. Then there's the shop and all the stock. That's worth quite a lot.'

'You don't know yet how much the kidnappers are eventually going to ask for,' Benedict pointed out. 'This five thousand is only a first demand. The final amount they ask for is certainly going to be very much more.'

'It doesn't matter how much they ask for. I'll find it!' she said stormily.

'You're not going to be able to come up with five thousand by eleven o'clock tomorrow morning.'

She turned away from him so that he couldn't see the tears of frustration welling up in her eyes. He was absolutely right, of course. She *couldn't* come up with that amount at such short notice. She wasn't even sure that she could raise it if they gave her a couple of weeks.

Benedict caught hold of her arm and swung her back to face him. 'Let me pay the money,' he repeated. 'I can easily get hold of that amount.'

'No,' she repeated with fierce stubbornness.

'You don't really have any choice,' he pointed out.

She knew that. And she hated it.

Benedict looked at her through narrowed eyes. 'Why are you behaving like this?'

She gazed straight back at him, her green eyes overbright and angry.

'Because I'm sick of all of this. I just want to hand over the money, get Angeline back, and then get away from here! But instead we've got to play more games, wait for more phone-calls and letters—it just goes on and on, and *I've had enough*. I hate all this intrigue. I like things to be open and straightforward. And I hate the thought of that man—that kidnapper— coming so close to me. He must have brushed right up against me to put that note in my bag. I didn't notice him, but he was right there beside me! Perhaps he even touched me.' She shivered violently. 'I want this to be over!' she finished on a fierce note.

Benedict's own gaze remained level. 'This is only going to be over if we go along with the kidnappers' demands, and do exactly as they say. We also need to keep our heads. It isn't going to help anyone if we start getting hysterical.'

'You mean, if *I* start getting hysterical,' Amy muttered in a tense voice. 'Nothing gets to you, does it? Always so calm, always so in control. You function like a robot—and you've probably got the same total lack of feelings!'

She had no idea why she was saying all these things and reacting like this. She supposed the tension inside of her had just boiled up to the point where it had to explode in some way. And the thought of that kidnapper coming so close to her really had spooked her.

They were still standing on the viewing-platform of the Galata Tower, and their raised voices had begun to attract attention.

'Let's get out of here,' Benedict muttered, seizing hold of her arm and propelling her towards the door.

'Let go of me!' she hissed at him. 'I don't want you touching me.'

His fingers released her immediately. At the time, a black expression crossed his face. Amy saw it, and knew that she was pushing him too far. She couldn't seem to help it, though. Or stop it.

They went down in the lift in silence, glaring hostilely at each other. Then they were back out in the hot, crowded, noisy streets.

'Where are you going?' Amy demanded, as Benedict began to stride off.

'To the bank,' he informed her curtly. 'I have to make the arrangements to draw out the money to pay the ransom.'

That brought her back to some kind of reality. 'The ransom,' she echoed slowly. It reminded her that, although she wasn't enjoying life in the least at the moment, her cousin was very much worse off. Angeline had lost her freedom, and was probably living in constant terror.

A great wave of shame swept through Amy. Why on earth was she indulging in petty bouts of temper, when she ought to be concentrating on raising the money that would buy Angeline's freedom? Feeling thoroughly disgusted with herself, she hurried after Benedict, determined not to give him any more trouble.

He was some time at the bank, making the necessary financial arrangements. When he finally came out again, he looked thoughtful. 'The kidnappers asked to be paid in pounds,' he remarked. 'Not Turkish lira.'

Amy frowned. 'Is that significant?'

Benedict shrugged. 'I don't really know. But it's certainly interesting.'

She was about to retort that she didn't find any of this particularly interesting. At the last moment, though, she remembered her resolution not to cause more trouble, and held her tongue.

Since there didn't seem to be anything else they could do, they made their way slowly back to the hotel. Amy collected the key to her room—her new room that she wouldn't be sharing with anyone, and especially not with Benedict—and then trailed after him as he walked towards the lift.

Her room was actually quite close to his—just a couple of doors along the same corridor. She wasn't sure if she was pleased about that, or not. Part of her didn't want to be near him, and part of her couldn't bear to be too far away.

You're very mixed up, she warned herself shakily. And you had better sort yourself out before it's time to leave Istanbul. When Angeline's finally free, he'll be going back to England with her, not you.

It was amazing how even the thought of it caused her to flinch, as if she were in some kind of physical pain. She was just glad that Benedict was walking in front of her, so that he couldn't see her involuntary reaction.

When he reached his room—the room that they had shared until now—he stopped.

'The hotel porter should have moved your things,' he told her. 'But perhaps you'd better just check, to make sure he hasn't left anything behind.'

Amy didn't want to go in that room again, but she couldn't think of any plausible excuse for not checking that all of her things had been moved out. Benedict unlocked the door, opened it, and then stood aside so that she could go in.

Rather hurriedly, she looked through the cupboards and drawers.

'Yes, they've moved everything,' she said at last, a little breathlessly. 'I'd better go and get settled into my new room.'

She didn't move, though, and Benedict didn't step away from the doorway.

They stood there, just staring at each other, for what seemed to be a very long time. Then Benedict moved aside and Amy took advantage of the escape route that had been offered to her. She rushed past him to the safety of her own room, flopped down on to the bed, and silently prayed for enough strength to get through the next couple of days.

Somehow, she struggled through what was left of the day, and then tossed and turned through a long, sleepless night. It felt funny, being in a room on her own. That rather horrified her. Only a couple of nights sleeping in the same room as Benedict, and already she was used to it!

In the morning she felt tired and listless, and there were dark shadows around her eyes. Benedict took one look at her, and asked if she wanted him to go on his own to deliver the five thousand pounds. That was exactly what Amy wanted, but she was never going to admit it. Anyway, she owed it to Angeline to see this through to the very end.

It all went surprisingly smoothly. They reached the gardens of the Topkapi Palace exactly on time, and

left the money under the seat in the north corner.
There were a lot of people around, and Amy kept
glancing at their faces nervously. Any one of them
could be one of the kidnappers. They must be around
here somewhere, waiting to pick up the money.

The letter had told them to leave the money, and
then walk away without looking back. It was very hard
to do that. Amy didn't think that she could have re-
sisted the temptation to glance round if it hadn't been
for the hard pressure of Benedict's fingers on her arm.

They went straight back to the hotel. Without
thinking, she followed him into his room.

'What do we do now?' she asked edgily. 'Just sit
here and wait for another phone-call?'

'There's not much else we can do,' Benedict replied
briefly. For once, he seemed almost as nervous as she
was.

'I hate all this waiting,' she muttered. 'But I hate
it even more when something finally happens. I
suppose that sounds a little crazy.'

'This whole affair is beginning to seem rather crazy.'

Amy went to flick a silver-gold strand of her hair
back from her face, and discovered that her fingers
were trembling.

'I didn't realise I was *that* nervous,' she said with
a rather strained laugh.

'Perhaps you'd better sit down for a couple of
minutes,' Benedict suggested. 'I'll ring down for a
brandy, if you like.'

'No,' she said, her voice almost as shaky as her
hands, 'I'm fine.'

He moved a little closer. 'You're not fine at all.'

She stared down at her fingers again. 'I suppose I'm not. But I will be in a few minutes. I just need a little time to get myself together.'

'Is that really all you need?' he asked softly.

The abrupt change in his tone made her swiftly look up at him.

'What do you mean?' she asked guardedly.

'Sometimes I get the impression that it isn't just this business with Angeline that's making you so nervous. I think that it's also got something to do with me.'

Her heart and stomach jumped in unison—a fairly unpleasant sensation.

'You?' she repeated, with as much incredulity as she could manage—which wasn't much. 'Why on earth should you make me feel nervous?'

'That's what I'd rather like to know,' Benedict replied, his dark eyes fixing on her in a way that made her pulses thump faster with fresh anxiety. 'I'm beginning to come up with one or two theories, but I think that I need to test them before I reach any definite conclusion.'

'T-test them?' Her voice came out as a tense squeak this time, which rather frightened her. It was always dangerous to lose control when Benedict was around.

He moved still nearer. Amy jumped nervously to her feet, but then realised that that had been a wrong move. It brought her almost face to face with him.

'You're still shaking,' Benedict observed.

'That's hardly surprising, after the stresses and strains of the last couple of days,' she retorted. 'Anyone would shake, under those sort of circumstances.'

'Perhaps I can do something about it,' he offered.

'There's no need for you to do *anything*,' Amy shot back at once. 'I'll be all right in a minute. All I need to do is calm down a little.'

Which was almost impossible with him standing there, only inches away! She had to get out of here—and fairly quickly.

But he was blocking her escape route. She couldn't get past him without some rather awkward manoeuvring, which would make it very obvious that she was trying to run away from him.

I'll shift to one side, and then sidle out of the door, she decided, her breathing coming a little quicker. But slowly, even nonchalantly—if I can manage it! I *won't* run.

She had only taken one step, though, when Benedict's hand descended lightly on her arm.

'I think you should sit down again.'

'Why?' she shot back nervously.

'Your neck and shoulder muscles are knotted up with tension. I can do something about that.'

'I'm perfectly all right,' Amy insisted.

He didn't take any notice of her reply. Instead, his other hand gripped her shoulder; then, with one easy shove, he pushed her into the chair. He moved behind her, flicked her hair away from her neck, and then let his fingers begin to dig lightly into her clenched muscles.

The whole sequence of movements had been executed so quickly, so smoothly, that there didn't seem any point at which Amy could have stopped him. When he began to massage the tension away with expert hands, she opened her mouth to protest, but then closed it again. This was *nice*. Her muscles already felt as if they were melting into a state of relaxation. Perhaps it wouldn't hurt to let him carry on for just a couple more minutes.

'Close your eyes,' Benedict instructed softly.

Without thinking, she obeyed. His fingers slid smoothly over the line of her shoulders, tangled themselves briefly in the silk of her hair, as if they liked the soft touch of the silver-gold strands, and then rested for a few moments on the nape of her neck.

Amy's eyes began to flicker open again. Rather too late, she was realising that this *wasn't* a good idea. In fact, she must have been mad—or even more shaken and upset than she had realised—to let him get this close to her.

She began to get up, but his hands immediately tightened their grip on her shoulders and gently pressed down, keeping her exactly where she was.

'Don't move,' he said.

'But I want to,' Amy insisted.

'No, you don't.'

It annoyed her that he had said it with such certainty. Arrogant man! she thought, giving him a dark scowl. He's so certain that he knows what's going on inside my head. The really scary part, though, was that he *did* seem to know.

His hands remained where they were, and just his thumbs gently moved, lightly caressing the soft, vulnerable skin around her hairline. Amy had to work very hard to suppress an involuntary shiver. This was getting dangerous, she warned herself. Time to get out of here!

'I want you to let go of me,' she said in a very firm, clear voice.

To her astonishment, he instantly released her. For a couple of moments she just sat there, too surprised to move. Then she realised that she had better take advantage of her freedom, and hurriedly got to her feet.

As soon as she stood up, however, Benedict moved round so that he was facing her.

'This is better,' he said a little huskily. 'I can touch a great deal more of you now.'

Amy's nervous system gave a gigantic twitch of alarm. He had never had any intention of letting her get away. He had simply wanted her out of that chair so that he could—could—— Could do what? she wondered with a fresh flash of apprehension.

So that he could *kiss* her, she discovered an instant later, as his mouth smoothly descended on hers. For a big man, he could move so swiftly. She never seemed to have time to take evasive action. Or perhaps she didn't actually want to take it, because she had already discovered one fairly terrifying fact. She would give ten years of her life for just ten seconds of a kiss like this.

And it went on for a lot longer than ten seconds. In the end, it finished only because neither of them had any breath left. Benedict briefly raised his head, but she could tell from the dark blaze of his eyes and the flush along the line of his cheekbones that he had no intention of stopping for any longer than it took to draw a quick, deep breath.

This is the time to tell him that this isn't going any further, Amy told herself shakily. Do it *now*, before you get dragged any deeper into this.

But it was already too late. She had the feeling that it had been too late from the very moment when she had first set eyes on him.

He didn't—couldn't—feel the same way, of course. This was just a diversion for him—the release of all the built-up tension and frustration. That ought to be important; ought to be enough to make her turn and walk away, because it was humiliating only to be wanted as a substitute for someone else. And especially when that someone was your own cousin.

Then the next kiss began, and Amy knew that she was quite incapable of walking anywhere. If this was humiliation, then she was going to have to learn how to live with it. Right now she wanted, needed, craved this closeness.

His kisses became a fraction gentler, as if he sensed that there was very little fight left in her. At the same time he pulled her closer, coiled her round him, so that hot body pressed against hot body, skin softly rubbed against skin, and small flash-points of a very physical desire flared into life.

Benedict's hands slid under the thin material of her T-shirt, touched restlessly and then became still again, pausing just beneath the aching swell of her breasts.

'This isn't the way I thought it would be,' he muttered, and he sounded almost puzzled.

Amy didn't understand what he was talking about. She did know that his hands seemed to be burning right into her skin, though, and she bit her lip to stop herself begging for more of those destructive caresses.

Benedict hesitated for a moment longer, as if uncharacteristically uncertain where to go from here. Then he seemed unable to prevent himself from suddenly pulling her still closer, the powerful length of his body imprinting itself against hers, leaving invisible scorch marks that she was certain were going to be there for the rest of her life.

This time, his kisses were much rougher and more demanding, as if he now knew very well what he wanted from her and was single-mindedly determined to take it. Amy knew that she should be frightened half to death by this new assault, but fear was something that she seemed incapable of feeling any more—especially when he was this close. Instead, her body melted into his, provoking him into more demanding caresses. His mouth bruised her lips, but they were bruises of pleasure, not pain.

He lifted his head and the brilliant blaze of his eyes held an unspoken question. But Amy never knew what her answer would have been because, at that precise moment, the phone rang.

Very slowly, Benedict released her. Then, more abruptly, he turned away from her.

'You'd better answer it,' he said in a rather harsh voice.

Amy made an effort to control her breathing, and then picked up the receiver with a shaking hand.

'Hello?' she said in a low tone.

'Amy? Amy, is that you?'

In those couple of moments, everything else was forgotten. Amy clutched the receiver more tightly.

'Angeline?' she said incredulously. 'Is that really you? Are you all right? Are you free?'

'No,' said her cousin in a small, frightened voice. 'Please, just listen. They'll only let me speak for a few seconds, and they've told me what to say. I'm not hurt, and they've promised to let me go if you give them what they want. You mustn't do anything silly, though. You haven't been to the police, have you?' she went on, not quite able to control the note of panic that broke through.

'No, of course not,' Amy assured her immediately. 'And we will do whatever they want.'

She heard her cousin give a very audible sigh of relief. Then Angeline said very quickly, 'They're telling me to put the phone down. Pay them the money, Amy; *please* pay it. I'm so frightened——'

Then the phone abruptly went dead. Amy slowly replaced the receiver and knew that her face had gone quite ashen.

In a shaky voice, she told Benedict what Angeline had said.

'You're absolutely sure it was Angeline on the other end of the phone?' he asked with a small frown.

'Of course I'm sure! I know my cousin's voice well enough.'

'She didn't give any clue as to where she's being held?'

'How could she? The kidnappers were listening to everything she said, then they cut her off before she had even finished speaking.' She gave a small shiver. 'She sounded so scared,' she added, almost in a whisper.

'My guess is that the kidnappers will be in touch again fairly soon, with their final demand,' Benedict said in a matter-of-fact voice.

Amy suddenly rounded on him. 'How can you sound so calm? That was *Angeline* on the other end of the phone!'

'I know,' he said. His dark eyes suddenly flickered. 'And I'm not calm at the moment. But the reason I'm not calm has nothing to do with Angeline.'

Something in his tone of voice made Amy stare at him for an instant. Then she shook her head as a wave of disgust rolled over her.

'How can you say something like that? All we ought to be thinking about right now is Angeline!'

'Perhaps we've thought about Angeline quite enough these last few days. Maybe it's time we began to think about ourselves,' Benedict suggested.

But Amy was too riddled with guilt even to listen to him. 'Angeline is sitting at the other end of that phone, frightened out of her life, and what are we doing?' she demanded. 'We're playing games with each other. For a while, we completely forgot about her! Well, I don't know about you, but that makes me feel pretty sick. I didn't know I could do something like that.'

'I think there are a lot of things that you don't know about yourself,' Benedict said softly.

Amy raised her head and her green eyes shone brilliantly as she glanced at him.

'Perhaps they're the kind of things that I don't *want* to know about myself. Not if it means that I can forget how to be a decent, caring human being.'

'Don't become too obsessed with this business with your cousin,' Benedict warned. 'It won't help Angeline, and it isn't healthy.'

'Then what would you like me to become obsessed about?' she challenged him angrily. '*You?*'

They stared at each other, her blazing green eyes gazing straight into the dark, turbulent depths of his eyes. Then Amy somehow tore her gaze away again.

'I'm getting out of here,' she muttered. 'I don't like the kind of person I become when I'm near you!'

With that, she rushed out of the room, determined to put as much distance as she could between herself and Benedict Kane.

CHAPTER EIGHT

AMY didn't go to her own room. That was still far too near to Benedict. Instead, she ran down the stairs, through the lobby and out of the hotel.

Once she was out in the crowded streets of Istanbul, she just kept walking blindly. She took no notice of the crowds jostling past her, or the sun beating down hotly on her uncovered head. She just needed to keep moving, to stop thinking, to shut out the sound of Angeline's frightened voice, which kept echoing through her whirling head.

She had no idea where she was going. She turned corners, cut through alleyways, and rushed across roads, with little regard for the blaring of horns as she stepped out right in front of trucks and cars.

In the end, it was the heat that finally forced her to slow down. Her skin was moist with sweat, and when she saw a dark archway ahead she instinctively headed towards it.

Once she was out of the sun, a little common sense slowly began to return. Amy slowed down to a more moderate pace, and she began to take some notice of her surroundings.

She realised that the archway had led her into a huge building that was divided up into a labyrinth of alleyways and cul-de-sacs. They were dimly lit, crowded, and lined with shops that appeared to sell everything under the sun. After a few minutes, Amy realised that she had wandered into the Covered Bazaar.

She walked on and on, surrounded by a dazzling mixture of sights and sounds and smells. There were carpets in every conceivable colour and pattern; multi-coloured shawls; bolts of cloth in brilliant shades; the glitter of gold and the dull glow of pewter; the smell of vanilla and cloves and perfume; row after row of shoes; and clothes with fake designer-labels.

Amy wandered on through the narrow alleys, sometimes stopping for an instant to stare rather blankly into a shop, and then quickly moving on before the owner could rush out and try to sell her something. The Bazaar was packed with people—tourists looking for a bargain; porters bent nearly double under incredible loads; dark-haired, dark-eyed men; women with their heads shrouded in scarves; hawkers selling their wares in a dozen different languages. It was totally bewildering, and yet Amy felt safe there. She could lose herself in the jostling crowds, get swept away by the noise and colour and confusion, and stop thinking about everything else for a while.

Then a hand clamped down on to her shoulder. Before she had a chance to yell out in alarm, she had been swung round to face the man who had accosted her. Like so many of the men in the Bazaar, he was dark-haired and dark-eyed. Unlike them, however, he was totally familiar to her.

Benedict's gaze locked on to hers. 'Where the hell do you think you're going?' he asked tightly.

'I don't think that's any business of yours,' Amy retorted, a nervous edge to her voice.

'You've been wandering around the streets of Istanbul for most of the afternoon.'

'How do you know that?' she demanded. 'Have you been following me?'

'Yes.'

His flat answer made her even more angry. 'Why?' she asked furiously. 'Believe it or not, I am old enough to go out on my own!'

'It isn't a good idea to walk around by yourself in a strange city. It could be dangerous.'

'That's funny,' Amy retorted. 'I thought it was pretty dangerous to be anywhere near *you*!'

'You're right; there is something dangerous going on between us,' he agreed in a grimmer tone. 'And I think it's time that we finally got it settled.'

He gripped hold of her arm again, and she threw a black look at him. 'What do you think you're doing?'

'Taking you back to the hotel.'

'No, you're not!'

He was already forcing her to move, though—still holding her arm very tightly, and pushing her forward.

'Let go of me!' she hissed at him.

'Not until we're out of here,' Benedict replied implacably, marching her towards one of the exits from the Bazaar.

'If you don't let go my arm, I'll scream,' she threatened.

'Go ahead,' he invited. 'But remember that this is a Muslim country. Woman are still expected to be subservient to men. It's highly unlikely that anyone will try and stop me doing whatever I like with you.'

Amy glanced around with widening eyes. In this part of the Bazaar, there were a great many men and very few women. Some of the men were watching as Benedict hauled her along, and she could clearly see a mixture of amusement and approval on their faces at the way Benedict was treating her.

'Just wait until the feminist movement gets going in this country,' she yelled at them fiercely. 'That'll wipe the smug smiles off your faces!'

Although they probably hadn't understood a word she had said, their grins grew wider and a couple of them called out encouragingly to Benedict as he continued to drag her forcefully out of the Bazaar.

Amy could have wept in pure frustration. The only thing that stopped her was an absolute determination not to let even a single tear fall in front of all these laughing, arrogant men.

They finally left the Bazaar, and she let out a shaky sigh of relief. It looked as if this ordeal was nearly over.

But Benedict didn't let go of her. Instead, he marched her on through the narrow, crowded streets.

'Where are you taking me?' she demanded.

'I've already told you that. Back to the hotel.'

'You said you'd let me go once we were out of the Bazaar. But you're still holding on to me,' she said accusingly.

'Yes, I am,' Benedict agreed.

Amy realised that she was rather unnerved by his tone of voice. There was a steely forcefulness to it, as if he had reached some decision and was absolutely determined to go through with it.

She tried to wriggle free, but it was no good; there was no way that she could get away from the iron grip of his fingers. She thought of yelling for help, but she was just too embarrassed. People were already staring at her with some curiosity. She didn't want to draw even more attention to herself. Anyway, she had already decided that it didn't really matter if Benedict dragged her back to the hotel. She had had enough of walking around Istanbul. She was tired, her feet ached, and she longed for a cool shower and a long sleep.

When the hotel finally came into sight, Amy let out a sigh of relief. In a couple of minutes, she would be back to her room. She could lock her door on Benedict Kane, and try to forget about him for a few hours.

They went up in the lift in silence. Amy glared angrily at Benedict a couple of times, but he didn't even look back at her. When they reached the door to his room, though, instead of letting her walk on to her own room, Benedict caught hold of her arm again, shoved her inside, and then closed and locked the door behind her.

'What are you doing *now*?' she said furiously, but with a new note of apprehension in her voice. His dark eyes glowed with a light that she hadn't seen before, and there was an alarmingly determined set to his mouth.

'I'm going to finish what we started earlier,' he informed her. 'I think that it's time we both understood what is going on here.'

'I don't want to understand one single thing about you,' Amy retorted. 'And I certainly don't want to be locked in this room with you!'

His gaze caught and held hers, its darkness intensifying still further. 'But I think that you do,' he said softly. 'I think that's *exactly* what you want.'

A cold shiver rippled right up Amy's spine. She managed to keep control of her voice, though. 'You're so arrogant,' she threw at him scornfully. 'You really think you're irresistible—that you've only got to click your fingers and you can have anyone you want. Well, you can click your fingers at me for a week, and I still won't want to come anywhere near you!'

'Liar,' he said evenly.

'Don't you dare call me a liar!'

'You want to be in this room with me,' Benedict said with absolute certainty.

Amy had to fight very hard to suppress another shiver. 'I don't want to be with you and I don't want anything from you,' she denied fiercely.

'Yes, you do,' he said, his eyes almost black now. 'You want this.'

She supposed she had known all along that she was going to have to fight him. What she hadn't known was how short-lived that fight was going to be.

Just one long, deep, overwhelming kiss, and all of her defences were undermined. Another kiss, shorter yet fiercer, and they began to fall apart.

Benedict raised his head and drew in an unsteady breath. '*Do* you want to be with me?' he challenged roughly.

'No,' she managed to mutter, but in a voice that said the very opposite.

The next kiss demolished the last frail shreds of her defiance.

'Do you?' Benedict repeated. 'I want to hear you say it!'

'Yes,' Amy found herself whispering, although she couldn't quite believe she had given in so quickly and so easily.

He relaxed just a fraction. 'And I want to be with you,' he murmured. 'I'm only just beginning to realise how much.'

His hands delved down under her T-shirt, as if impatient for the touch of her against his palms, his fingertips.

Amy shuddered, and fought to cling on to the faint shadows of common sense. 'We can't do this. *I* can't do it. It isn't right. Especially not now, when we ought to be thinking only of Angeline.'

'I haven't forgotten Angeline. But right at this moment, this is the only thing that seems important.'

'It can't be!' Amy said a little frantically.

'Then tell me that it *isn't* important.'

But she couldn't do that. Instead, she half turned away from him. 'This is only sex,' she muttered at last. 'Just something that's happened because we've been thrown together in difficult circumstances.'

'No, it isn't,' Benedict said with complete certainty. 'I've had a couple of affairs that were like that: a flare-up of physical attraction that lasted a few weeks and then burned itself out. This isn't anything like that.'

'Then what *is* it like?' she said in an almost frightened voice.

'I don't know,' he replied simply. 'It's new to me, as well. But I do know that I like it,' he went on more huskily.

He reached for her again, and there was a new purpose in the movements of his hands. They skimmed over her as if needing to acquaint themselves with the outline of her body before delving into her more intimate secrets.

Amy briefly closed her eyes. During the one brief and disastrous affair she had had during her adult life, she had thought that she had known what sex and passion was all about. Now she realised that she hadn't known anything about it at all. It wasn't just touching, the pleasant warmth and closeness of another body, and then a vaguely unsatisfactory and too-quick ending. It was a flaring of every nerve-end, the knowledge that it had to be *this* body close to hers and no other, the quickening of pulses and the heavy thump of an erratic heartbeat. More than anything, it was a need that she could see stretching on and on to the end of her life—a need that wasn't simply physical, but something much more complex, deep and frightening in its intensity.

Benedict looked down at her for a few moments. Then he suddenly smiled. 'It's going to be all right,' he said with total confidence. Then his mouth closed over hers and everything began to happen very fast.

His arms slid round her and pulled her very close. She could feel the heat of his body burning through the thin material of his shirt. Her fingers dug into his skin, as if she desperately needed something to hold on to, and he made a small sound in his throat, as if her involuntary response pleased him.

Seconds later, they were lying side by side on the bed. Amy had no idea how she had got there; she didn't remember moving of her own accord, but neither did she remember being lifted. Benedict's hands were already moving again, and he seemed to be having difficulty in controlling their eagerness. They slid beneath her clothes, lightly nipped and then caressed, delved deeper, and caused her to catch her breath before surfacing again, this time to begin impatiently to remove her clothes.

Amy managed a small shake of her head. 'I—I don't behave like this,' she mumbled rather incoherently. 'I don't hop into bed with someone I've only known for a few days.'

Benedict's dark gaze fixed on her face. 'We're not "hopping into bed",' he said with an unexpected trace of anger.

'Then w-what are we doing?'

'We're getting to know each other in every way possible.'

'Why?'

'Damn it, do you always ask so many questions at such an inconvenient time?' he murmured. He finished pulling off her T-shirt and stared hungrily for a few moments at the softness of her breasts, still constrained by the thin cotton of her bra. 'You want to know why we're doing this?' Benedict went on in a barely controlled voice, his fingers already searching for the clip that would release the warm fullness of her breasts into his hands. 'I can't give you an answer that makes any sense.' His tone became more husky as his palms finally covered her exposed, fair, baby-soft flesh. 'I only know that I want you in a very different way from all the ways I've wanted women in the past.' His fingers lingered for a few more moments, lightly rubbing the pale pink of her nipples into an aching hardness, and then reluctantly moving on to deal with the waistband of her jeans. 'I can't even tell you when this started,' he went on, his voice a lot less steady now. 'Perhaps the moment I first saw you. Or perhaps not until I really looked at you for the first time and realised that you didn't look like

Angeline; you didn't look like anyone except Amy Stewart. Someone quite unique. Someone who seemed able to get to me in ways that I didn't even know existed until you walked into my life.' He unzipped her jeans. 'Raise your hips,' he ordered softly.

In numbed silence, Amy obeyed. He slid off her jeans, and then let his hands trail along the long length of her legs. She shivered violently as the sensitive skin of her thighs responded to his heated touch, and he made it clear that he liked being able to provoke such a response in her.

Her own hands began to touch, rather hesitantly at first, but then more quickly, more restlessly, as her palms started to crave the light friction of his skin against hers. He slid off his clothes so that she could explore further. Her fingers ached with the pleasure of this intimate contact with him. His skin was smooth and supple, his muscles hard and a little tense as he struggled to hold on to some vestiges of control.

'No more,' he said tightly at last. 'Not for a few moments.'

He slid back from her and took a couple of very deep, shuddering breaths. Amy discovered that she didn't want to be apart from him, not even for a few seconds. She slid after him, her body instinctively pressing against his. She had had no idea that she could behave like this; that it could feel so deliciously wicked and yet so right to want someone so very badly.

Benedict gave a small groan. 'Do you know what you're doing to me?'

'Yes, I know,' Amy whispered.

Her fingers lightly stroked and teased. His body was hot and hard now, every inch of him responsive to her touch. He gave another groan, and let his own hands have their way, exploring wherever they wanted to go. They moved over the soft curves, slid into the warm, dark niches, provoked small bursts of pleasure and then more lingering waves that rushed over her, leaving her hot and shaking.

Benedict bent his head to her breasts, his tongue licking, his teeth lightly nipping, tasting her, as if it were a sweet flavour that he never wanted to forget. Then his mouth closed over hers for a kiss that was quite unlike all the others he had given her—hard and fierce, totally possessive, as if he was demanding a small piece of her soul from her. And Amy gave it willingly. She knew now that she would give him anything, and forever.

When the kiss was finally over, Benedict stared down at her for a long time. Then, with a grunt of sheer frustration, he moved away from her.

'This is where we stop,' he said in a rough voice.

Amy began to emerge from the shroud of pleasure that had enveloped her. 'Stop?' she echoed in a soft, shaken tone. 'Don't—don't you want me?'

'Look at me,' he instructed. Amy felt the colour steal into her face as her eyes slid over his still aroused body. 'Do I *look* as if I don't want you? But if we snatch all the pleasure now, it'll leave nothing for later. And I don't want to rush this. It's important that we get it right. Do you understand?'

'I—I think so.'

Benedict leaned forward, caught hold of her and gave her a gentle shake.

'It's no good going too far, too fast. Until we understand what's happening between us, we need to take it at an easy pace.'

'Then—what was this all about?'

'I told you, I wanted to get to know more about you.' He gave a faint grin. 'And this was one way of doing it.'

'And what did you find out?' she asked him cautiously.

'A lot more than I expected.' Benedict's grin broadened. 'And you know a lot more about me, too. But it went rather further than I meant it to. You're turning out to be *very* irresistible.' He slid off the bed. 'In fact, I'm going to have to take a long, cold shower, or I'm not going to be in a fit state to go out in public!'

He disappeared into the bathroom, and Amy sat on the bed for a while, her knees drawn up to her chin and her teeth gently chattering with reaction. She had never expected anything like this. She wasn't at all sure that she knew what to do about it, how to handle it. One thing was certain, though. Benedict now knew *exactly* how she felt about him. And the extraordinary thing was that he seemed to like it.

Very slowly, Amy pulled her clothes back on. Her skin still seemed almost painfully sensitive, and she shivered a little as she remembered how it had felt when Benedict had taken those same clothes off.

She could hear the shower running in the bathroom, and for just a moment, she thought of making a run for it before he came out again. This was too scary; too real. Then she gave a small, shaky sigh. This wasn't something that she was going to be able to run away from.

Benedict came out of the bathroom a few minutes later, and gave her a slow smile that seemed to make her bones melt.

'I think the cold shower was only a very temporary solution,' he said rather huskily. 'Perhaps we'd better not take this *too* slowly.'

'I wish I knew what was going on,' she said, almost in a whisper.

'So do I. It's surprised me as much as it has you. A few days ago, I didn't even know you existed. Now I'm beginning to feel as if I've known you forever.'

He sounded baffled, but quite cheerful, as if he was beginning to realise that he very much liked whatever it was that was happening between them. There was also a darkening glow in his eyes that warned Amy that the cold shower was already beginning to wear off.

At that moment, though, the phone suddenly began to ring shrilly. Amy jumped, and Benedict swore softly under his breath, as if deeply irritated by the interruption.

'You'd better answer it,' he said, rather abruptly.

Amy picked up the receiver. 'Ready for your final instructions?' said a male voice in her ear.

A wave of shame shot through her as she realised that, for a while, she had forgotten all about Angeline. Benedict seemed to have the ability to make her forget about everything except his own existence.

'Yes, I'm ready,' she said in a low voice.

'Tomorrow, take the early morning ferry from the Galata Bridge up the Bosporus. You'll only be going as far as the first stop, just before the Dolmabahçe Mosque. And you're to come alone. Leave your boyfriend at the hotel. Someone will be watching to make sure that he stays there. Oh, and one more thing,' he said with sudden, malicious humour. 'You'll need to bring some money with you. Sixty thousand pounds, to be exact. And make sure it's all there, or your cousin definitely won't enjoy the consequences.'

'I can't get that amount of money!' Amy said in growing panic.

'You've known all along that you were going to have to pay out a large amount to get your cousin back,' said the man implacably. 'You should have made all the necessary arrangements. And we're not prepared to bargain on this. Be on that ferry tomorrow morning, or you won't be hearing from us—or your cousin—again.'

Before Amy could say anything more, he put down the phone and cut the connection between them.

She turned to Benedict, her face absolutely colourless. 'They want sixty thousand pounds tomorrow morning. And I haven't got it! If I sold every single share that my uncle left me, then I'd just about be able to raise that amount, but there isn't time, and anyway, the trustees won't *let* me sell the shares.'

Benedict frowned. 'I wonder if it's just a coincidence that they're asking for almost exactly the same amount that your uncle left you?'

'You think that someone found out about it? That they snatched Angeline because it was a way of getting their hands on my uncle's money?' Then Amy shook her head impatiently. 'It isn't important now. It's getting the sixty thousand pounds that's the problem. It's just impossible!'

'No, it isn't,' Benedict said calmly.

'What do you suggest we do?' she retorted edgily. 'Print it?'

'We go to the bank first thing in the morning and draw it out.'

'That's all very well in theory, but I don't think they're going to let me run up that big an overdraft!'

'You don't have to. When I first visited the bank here, I made arrangements to draw out a large sum, if necessary. The money's there, waiting for us. All we have to do is collect it.'

Amy stared at him. 'You'd pay out sixty thousand pounds of your own money to get Angeline back again?'

His dark gaze locked on to hers. 'Yes—but not because she means anything to me. There was a time when I thought she might, but I was wrong about that. Over the last few days, I've realised just how wrong I was.'

She flushed a little at the implication behind his words. Then she muttered, 'I suppose I ought to tell you that I won't let you do this, that I won't take your money. But if I do that, then something terrible might happen to Angeline. But I'll pay it back; every single penny. I'll find some way to get round the legal restrictions, and sell those shares my uncle left me.'

'I don't want you to sell anything or pay me back. It really isn't important if it's your money or mine that pays for Angeline's release. There *is* something that's important, though, and that's your safety. I'm not going to let you go on that ferry on your own in the morning,' he warned her. 'I intend to stay very close by.'

'No, you can't do that,' she said at once. 'They'll be watching; they'll see you. Then Angeline will be in real danger.'

His eyebrows drew together lightly as he considered that problem. Then he gave a small, confident nod.

'Wait here,' he said, heading towards the door. 'I'll be back in about an hour.'

'Where are you going?' she called after him. He didn't answer, but simply shot a quick grin at her and then left.

She wandered restlessly round and round the room after he had gone. Everything kept happening far too fast. She felt totally confused now. And she had the feeling that she was going to remain confused for the rest of her life!

Just over an hour later, there was a light tap on the door. Amy gave a small groan. Who was it? She didn't feel like facing anyone right now.

She opened the door and flicked a quick glance at the tall man who stood outside. She didn't recognise him, and she scowled. 'You've got the wrong room——' she began. Then she blinked, and looked again. *'Benedict?'* she said faintly.

He was wearing old workmen's clothes, he had had his hair cut in a different style, and he was wearing a false moustache!

'If *you* didn't recognise me, then neither should the kidnappers,' he said cheerfully.

'You look—very Turkish,' Amy said in amazement.

'That's the general idea. And I've got some tanning lotion to make my skin even darker. The ferry should be fairly crowded in the morning. I'll mix with the other locals on board, and the kidnappers shouldn't notice or recognise me.'

'This is crazy,' Amy muttered with a rather dazed shake of her head. 'In fact, the whole thing's crazy!'

Benedict pulled off the false moustache, and suddenly looked much more like himself. 'The last few days have certainly been—different,' he agreed drily.

She let out a deep sigh. 'If only Angeline weren't in such danger. It casts a great black shadow over everything.'

'Perhaps you should stop worrying about your cousin quite so much,' suggested Benedict.

'How can I do that?' she demanded rather indignantly.

'Just remember that she's the kind of girl who's very good at looking after her own interests.'

'She's not in any *position* to look after her own interests,' Amy pointed out a little angrily. 'She's a prisoner!'

Benedict seemed about to say something, but then stopped himself. He turned away for a couple of moments, then swung back and said in a rather different tone of voice, 'It's getting late; we'd better go down and have dinner. Then we'll try and get some sleep. Tomorrow's going to be a difficult day.'

'Every day's been difficult since we came to Istanbul,' she muttered.

He moved closer. 'And so have the nights,' he said in a more husky tone.

She was suddenly certain that he was going to kiss her, and she instinctively moved away. She couldn't handle any more right now. Too much had happened, and too quickly. Her nerves were stretched to the point where they could all too easily snap apart.

A dark expression flickered across Benedict's face. 'I don't like it when you turn away from me,' he warned softly.

'A few days ago you didn't like it when I was near you!' she reminded him curtly.

'You're wrong about that. I think that I've always liked having you near me. What rattled me was the way I was beginning to feel about you.'

'I still don't *know* how you feel about me,' Amy said tightly.

'Oh, yes, you do.' His eyes began to glow again. 'I haven't told you, but you do know.'

He moved closer again and her lower lip suddenly began to tremble. 'We—we were going down to dinner,' she reminded him shakily.

'To hell with dinner.' His hands reached out for her and found her. 'To hell with everything,' he growled, and his eyes were almost black now as they shone at her hotly. 'I know that I said it was too soon, and it is and I'm sorry; but I don't seem to have any control over this, and I need you *now*.'

His mouth closed over hers almost before he had finished speaking, but it didn't matter; there wasn't anything that Amy wanted to say to him. Nothing she *could* say to him. She had suddenly run completely out of words.

Clothes were torn away hungrily, hot, damp skin rubbed against hot damp skin, and breathing became difficult, almost impossible. Everything suddenly seemed to be happening at a bewildering speed, and she plunged straight downwards into a dark pool of pleasure, every touch provoking a small gasp, desire dancing along over-sensitive nerve-ends and setting them alight, everything happening so fast and yet with a natural, sensual rhythm. Limbs coiled around limbs and seemed to merge, so that it was almost impossible to tell where female softness ended and male hardness began. She had had no idea that it was possible to want someone quite so much.

Benedict became caught up in the tangled bed-clothes, muttered something under his breath, and shook himself free. For just an instant, he remained very still as he gazed down at her, his eyes burning, his cheekbones flushed with colour.

'I want *you*,' he said very clearly. 'No one else. Just you.'

Amy stared straight back at him, and she had no idea what he could see in her eyes, but a moment later he moved again and there was a sudden darkness, heat and pressure, and a totally new surge of pleasure.

Everything after that became a jumble of vivid sensations. She tumbled on downwards and held on very tightly to Benedict because he seemed to be the only solid thing in a world that had turned into a turmoil of feelings and frantically moving bodies and small explosions of exquisite delight. Then the final great shudder that ran through him continued right on into the depths of her own body; the depths of her soul. She melted completely into him, shivered again and again with the force of the dark, hot pleasure that swept over her, and finally drifted on to a warm, sunlit plateau where everything seemed bathed in utter peace.

It was a very long time before Benedict finally raised his head again and looked down at her.

'All right?' he said quietly.

Amy couldn't seem to answer. Instead, she curled a little closer and buried her face against his shoulder.

He lightly stroked the nape of her neck. 'Sorry that it happened so fast. That it happened at all. I never meant it to. At least, not yet. What the hell are you doing to me?'

'I don't know,' she managed to say.

'Yes, you do,' Benedict said more gently. His fingers tangled themselves in the damp, gold strands of her hair and then comfortably remained there.

Amy closed her eyes, thought that she had never felt quite this happy in her entire life, and then slid into a deep, dreamless sleep.

CHAPTER NINE

When Amy woke up in the morning, they were both lying in exactly the same position.

'Oh,' she said out loud. And then, even more apprehensively, *'Oh.'*

Benedict stirred beside her. 'Oh, indeed,' he agreed in a relaxed voice. 'Things seem to be moving a lot faster than either of us intended. How do you feel about that?'

'I feel——' she began in a rather wobbly voice. Then, quite suddenly, everything seemed to be absolutely all right and she broke into a big smile. 'Right now, I feel very good,' she admitted.

'And in the future, you're going to feel even better,' he said comfortably.

Her green eyes opened very wide. 'How do you know that?'

'Because that's the kind of relationship this is going to be,' Benedict said with utter confidence. 'We both seem to have found something that we've been looking for for a long time. And we're going to hold on to it, and make very sure that it works.'

'Oh,' said Amy, yet again. Then she suddenly untangled herself from the warmth of his body and sat up very straight. 'Angeline,' she said, in a completely different tone of voice. 'We've forgotten all about Angeline!'

'I wish we could forget about her,' growled Benedict.

Her gaze flashed angrily. 'How can you say something like that?'

'On a morning like this, it's very easy, he replied drily. 'But I suppose we'd better get up and dressed, and deliver the money to the kidnappers.'

'If it's too much trouble, just stay in bed and I'll do it myself,' Amy said, glaring down at him.

'Are you angry with me?' he asked, his dark eyes drifting over her lazily. 'Yes, you are. It doesn't matter, though. I don't want you to be sugar and spice and all things nice, all the time. Nice girls are boring girls. I want you to be prickly, stubborn, independent—although you can be sweet to me in bed,' he added with a totally wicked grin.

'Angeline—and the money,' she reminded him, with some exasperation.

Benedict hauled himself out of bed. 'Want to share a shower?' he invited, his eyes gleaming. 'No, perhaps not,' he decided with obvious reluctance. 'Or we could spend the rest of the day discovering what fun you can have in a bathroom.'

Amy somehow dragged her gaze away from his strong, healthy body. His very *familiar* body, she reminded herself, a great blush surging up into her face.

Luckily, he had already disappeared into the bathroom and hadn't seen it. With a huge effort, she forced herself to stop thinking about everything that had happened since yesterday. This morning you've got to think about Angeline, she reminded herself. Everything else must wait. Getting Angeline back safely is the only thing of any importance right now.

While Benedict was in the bathroom, she scuttled back to her own room and hurriedly showered and dressed. Then there was just time for them to grab a quick breakfast. Amy was starving, and she realised that it was a long time since she had last had a meal. They had missed out on dinner last night. Then she remembered all over again *why* they had missed dinner, and spent a frantic few seconds trying to beat back the hot flush that threatened to engulf her.

Once they had finished eating, they headed straight for the bank. Benedict was inside for some time, and when he finally emerged, he was carrying a small briefcase.

'They lent me this to put the money in,' he said with a faint grin. 'They didn't want me to walk round the streets of Istanbul with sixty thousand pounds stuffed into my pockets.'

Amy stared at the briefcase nervously. Very soon she was going to have to hand it over to the kidnappers, and just the thought of it made her knees shake.

You're doing this for Angeline, she reminded herself a little crossly, annoyed at her own cowardice. All you've got to do is stay calm, obey their instructions, and everything will go smoothly.

Benedict handed over the briefcase. Then his face became more serious. 'I'm going back to the hotel now,' he told her. 'You'd better walk down to the dock and book your ticket for the ferry. And don't worry about anything. When you get on that boat, I'll be close behind you.'

'You're sure the kidnappers won't recognise you?' she said uneasily.

'You didn't, did you?' he reminded her with a brief smile.

'No, I didn't,' she admitted. 'All right, I'll see you later. And don't forget the false moustache!'

Her nervous attempt at humour fell rather flat, and when Benedict began to walk away from her, she felt an almost irresistible urge to run after him.

Don't be so gutless! she lectured herself angrily. Remember Angeline, waiting for you to hand over the money so that she can be set free.

With a small toss of her head that sent her gold-blonde hair rippling back over her shoulders, she began to walk determinedly in the direction of the Galata Bridge.

As always, the area around the Bridge was crammed with people, and it took her a while to push through the crowds, and even longer to find the right ticket window. Amy began to panic. What if she missed the ferry? What if Benedict couldn't get here on time and she had to go on the boat alone? What if——?

She closed her eyes for a couple of seconds, took a very deep breath, and somehow managed to calm herself. A few minutes later, she was clutching her ticket. And soon after that she was actually on board the ferry.

The boat was packed with people. Amy glanced around with newly raw nerves. Any one of them could be one of the kidnappers. And where was Benedict? She couldn't see him, and the ferry was almost ready to pull out.

You're not meant to see him, she reminded herself. Just as the kidnapper isn't meant to know he's on board.

She was too restless to sit down. Anyway, most of the seats were already full. In the end, she pushed her way over to the rail and stood staring at the unforgettable skyline of Istanbul as the ferry slowly chugged off down the Bosporus.

She knew that it wouldn't take long to reach the first ferry-stop. She could already see the square bulk of the Dolmabahçe Mosque, topped by its dome and flanked by two tall, thin minarets. What was going to happen? she wondered apprehensively. Was the kidnapper on the boat, or was he going to be waiting for her when she got off the ferry?

Just at that moment, a man's voice murmured in her ear. 'Don't turn round,' he instructed. 'Keep looking straight ahead, as if you're admiring the view.'

Amy recognised the voice at once. It was the man who had spoken to her on the phone, telling her what she had to do if she wanted her cousin to be set free.

Her muscles went quite rigid with tension, and she did exactly as he had ordered, staring in front of her, although without seeing anything.

'You're going to hand me that briefcase you're carrying,' the man went on in the same even tone, standing directly behind her so that she couldn't see him at all, only hear his voice. 'Then, as soon as the ferry docks, you're going to get off and go back to your hotel. And you're not going to look back, not even once, because it will be a lot safer for both you and your cousin if you don't see my face. Understand?'

Amy jerkily nodded her head.

'Fine,' said the man, with some satisfaction. 'Now—give me the briefcase.'

She held it out behind her, and felt someone take it from her. Then she heard it being opened as the man quickly checked the contents.

'That looks as if it's the right amount,' he said, sounding pleased. 'As soon as I'm in a safe place, I'll count it. Provided it's all there, to the last pound, you should soon be able to see your cousin.'

'When?' said Amy quickly. 'How?'

'I'll phone you and tell you where you can pick her up. Now, no more talking. The ferry's about to dock. Get off, and remember what I told you about not looking back.'

Amy moved forward on shaky legs. There was a large crowd of tourists disembarking from the ferry, ready to explore the Mosque and the splendours of the Dolmabahçe Palace, that lay just beyond. She got off with them, but then stayed on the quayside as the tourists walked on towards the Mosque.

She heard the ferry chugging away again, but she didn't turn round until the sound of its engine had completely faded. Benedict hadn't got off the ferry, so she guessed that he was still on board, shadowing the kidnapper. She just prayed that he would be very careful. Men like that could be totally ruthless.

There wasn't anything that she could do after that except wait for a ferry that would take her back to the Galata Bridge. Waiting was probably the hardest thing in the world to do, she decided edgily, as she paced up and down the quay. If only Benedict were here with her, instead of on that ferry! She felt as if she really needed him right now.

A ferry finally came along, and she hurried on board. As soon as it docked, Amy rushed back through the crowded streets to the hotel. Perhaps Benedict would be waiting there for her. Perhaps the phone was already ringing, telling her where she could find Angeline.

But the room was empty and the phone was silent. Amy flopped down on to the bed and gazed up at the ceiling for a couple of minutes. Then she was on her feet again, unable to keep still, roaming restlessly round and round the room, and occasionally staring out of the window.

It was nearly three hours before Benedict at last returned, and by then Amy was a total nervous wreck. As soon as he walked in the door, she flung herself at him, as if she were drowning and he was a lifebelt.

He held her very tightly, and didn't seem to mind that she was very nearly squeezing him to death. Then he swiftly kissed her.

'Oh, that tickles!' she said, startled back to reality.

'Sorry, I forgot I was still wearing it,' Benedict said with a grin. He tore off the false moustache and tossed it into the bin. 'I promise never to grow one.'

Amy felt much better now that he was here, and so close.

'What did you find out?' she asked. 'Were you on the ferry? I didn't see you. Did you follow the kidnapper? Do you know where Angeline is?'

'The answer to all those questions is "yes",' he said, and the smile had now disappeared from his mouth. 'Just let me change back into my own clothes, and then I'll take you to your cousin.'

'Is she all right?' Amy demanded. 'How do you know where she is?'

'I followed the man who collected the money from you. He got off the ferry at the next stop, and then made his way back to Istanbul. He's staying at a hotel only a few blocks away from here.'

'But what about Angeline?' said Amy, with growing impatience. 'Where is *Angeline*?'

'No more explanations for now,' replied Benedict. His voice had changed and, for some reason that she didn't understand, sounded harder. 'Give me a couple of minutes to change. Then I'll take you to the hotel where the kidnapper's staying.'

He shrugged off the workman's clothes, disappeared into the bathroom to wash the tanning lotion from his face and hands, and then pulled on jeans and a sweatshirt. 'OK, let's go,' he said briefly.

Amy wanted to ask at least a dozen more questions, but something about the expression on his face stopped her. What was going on here? she wondered uneasily. She had the feeling that, whatever it was, she wasn't going to like it.

Once they were out of the hotel, Benedict began to walk quickly through the crowded, sun-drenched streets. Amy trotted along beside him, frowning to herself as she tried to work out why Benedict was behaving like this. He finally stopped outside a small hotel down a side-street.

'This is it,' he said.

'What do we do now?' asked Amy. 'Call the police?'

'No.' He seemed about to say something, stopped, then finally added, 'You might want to call them later. That's something you'll have to decide for yourself.'

'You're being very mysterious,' she said rather crossly.

'Sorry, but——' Again, he seemed on the verge of saying something more, and again he stopped himself. 'Let's go up,' he said briefly.

Amy looked at him warily. 'Are you sure it's safe?'

'Oh, yes,' he said, in the same rather hard tone that he had used earlier. 'I'm sure of that.'

She frowned as she followed him inside. What was this all about?

Benedict seemed to know exactly where he was going. He headed straight for the stairs, and then went directly up to the second floor. Finally, he stopped outside a room at the very end of the corridor.

'Your cousin is in here,' he said in a low voice.

Amy stared at him, startled. 'They've been keeping her prisoner in a hotel-room? Wasn't that risky? One of the hotel staff could easily have found out. They must come in to change the beds and clean the rooms.'

'Just open the door,' Benedict instructed. 'But do it very quietly.'

She shot him a puzzled look, but obeyed. She turned the handle very gently, and then stood silently in the doorway.

Almost at once, she heard a familiar voice. It was the man who had spoken to her on the phone; the man who had collected the money from her on the ferry.

'I never thought it would go so smoothly,' he said. 'You were right; it really was very easy.'

'Of course it was,' said the girl's voice, confidently. 'We worked everything out beforehand; there was no reason why it should go wrong. I'll admit that I nearly died when I found that she'd brought Benedict with her, but in the end it wasn't a problem. In fact it gave me quite a laugh when they concocted that story about Benedict being Amy's fiancé. And now we've got the money, we can go anywhere and do anything we want.'

Amy stood there absolutely frozen. It was *Angeline* who was speaking. Angeline, who wasn't being held a terrified prisoner by kidnappers. Angeline, who was sitting in this comfortable hotel-room, looking forward to spending sixty thousand pounds that didn't belong to her.

Quietly, she walked forwards, closely followed by Benedict. Angeline and the man with her were sitting on the far side of the room, and didn't notice them straight away. The money was piled up on a table in front of them, and Angeline was running her fingers through it in an almost sensual movement, her blue eyes gleaming.

Then she turned her head, and saw her cousin for the first time. She sat very still, and the bright glow left her eyes.

'Oh, hell,' she said flatly. 'And I was just beginning to think that we'd got away with it.'

Amy just stared at her. She couldn't seem to say anything.

Angeline was the first one to break the long, strained silence. 'Lost your tongue?' she enquired caustically. 'Aren't you going to threaten me with the police? Tell me you're going to have me charged with fraud? Or is it extortion?' She suddenly swung at the money angrily, scattering it on to the floor. 'Why didn't you come to Istanbul on your own?' she said fiercely. 'Why did you bring *him*?' She glared at Benedict with sudden hatred. 'He's so clever, I knew we were in trouble as soon as I found out he was here. I bet he knew right from the start that the whole thing was a put-up job.'

'No, I didn't,' Benedict answered tightly. 'Believe it or not, I came because I was genuinely concerned about your safety. Which proves that I'm not quite as clever as you seem to think I am,' he added, his dark eyes suddenly flashing. 'But then I gradually became suspicious. Things didn't quite seem to fit together. And when you asked for the exact amount of money that Amy had inherited from her uncle, I was fairly sure that this wasn't a genuine kidnapping.'

Amy swung round and stared at Benedict. 'You didn't tell *me* any of this,' she said in bewilderment. 'You let me go on thinking that Angeline was really in danger!'

'There was always a chance that I was wrong,' answered Benedict. 'And I knew that you were fond of your cousin. I didn't want to accuse her of anything until I was sure that I was right.'

Amy turned back to Angeline, still bewildered. 'Why did you do it?'

'Because I was cheated out of my share of Uncle's money,' Angeline said bitterly. 'I should have had half; I was *entitled* to half. Instead, every penny of it went to you. Good little Amy, sweet little Amy, everyone's favourite. You really make me sick, you know,' she went on vehemently. 'You always have done. So I decided to take the money away from you. I met Mike here when I came to Istanbul on holiday. Between us we came up with the idea of a phoney kidnapping, with the amount that Uncle left you being handed over as the ransom. And it nearly worked,' she said defiantly. 'We nearly got away with it.'

'Except that it wasn't Uncle's money that I handed over,' Amy told her in a slightly steadier voice. 'That sixty thousand pounds belongs to Benedict.'

Angeline's blue eyes widened, and she swung round to face Benedict. 'It's *your* money?' she said in astonishment.

'Amy's uncle laid down certain restrictions when he left her that inheritance,' Benedict said evenly. 'She can't touch any of the capital for five years.'

Angeline's gaze grew even wider. 'And so you paid the ransom? You just happened to have sixty thousand lying around? You've got that kind of money?' She gave a self-mocking laugh. 'I really messed up all round, didn't I? I should have stuck with you, and tried to hook you. You were a much better bet, in the long-term. I wasn't sure about you, though. There were rumours that you had money, but you never flashed it around. And anyway, I didn't think that I could go on pretending to be the kind of girl you thought I was. It was such an *effort*, being sweet and nice all the time. Pretending that I didn't care that all of Uncle's money had been left to Amy. I knew that I wouldn't be able to keep it up for much longer. That's why I decided to try and get my hands on Amy's inheritance, instead.' She stared directly at them, completely unrepentant about what she had done. 'So—what happens now?'

'For a start, we take back the money,' Benedict said coolly, gathering it together. 'As to what happens to you—that's up to Amy. Personally, I'd have the pair of you slung into gaol. She might feel slightly more charitable than me, though, as you're her cousin.'

'At the moment, I don't feel in the least charitable,' Amy said tightly. She was still finding it hard to believe that Angeline could have behaved in such an underhand, amoral way. She remembered all the anxiety, the sleepless nights she had gone through, and her mouth hardened still further. 'Let's get out of here,' she muttered to Benedict. 'If we stay any longer, I think I'm going to hit her!'

Afterwards, she couldn't remember anything of the walk back to the hotel. Once they reached their room, she flopped down into the nearest chair and shook her head, still feeling totally dazed.

'I knew that Angeline wasn't exactly a saint,' she said in a disbelieving voice. 'But I never thought she'd do anything like this!'

'She fooled me, too, for quite some time,' Benedict reminded her. 'And that isn't easy to do. Your cousin is very clever, in a rather twisted way.'

'I wish you'd told me when you started to suspect that the kidnapping was just a set-up,' Amy said, suddenly looking up at him.

'I told you, I wasn't sure. If I'd been wrong, then you'd have been very angry at me for even suggesting such a thing. And I didn't want you to be angry at me, at that particular time,' Benedict finished softly.

Something in his tone of voice made Amy swallow hard. She also began to realise that she wasn't nearly as furious and upset over this as she should have been. And the reason for that was very simple. There were too many other things to think about—and all of them centring on Benedict.

'Have you decided yet what you're going to do about Angeline?' he asked quietly.

Amy gave a rather helpless shrug. 'What *can* I do? What she did was criminal, but I can't go to the police and get her thrown into gaol. I just can't do it.'

'She deserves it,' Benedict reminded her a little grimly.

'I know that! But she's still my cousin, and despite everything she's done I feel slightly sorry for her. She's the real loser in all of this. She's behaved very badly, but she's got nothing out of it, and on top of all that——' Amy finally managed a very faint smile

'—she's lost you. She was right; you were the real prize. And now she will never have you.'

Benedict lifted one eyebrow slightly. 'I've never been described as a prize before!'

'Well, there's a first time for everything,' she said more cheerfully. Then she added, in a more serious tone, 'What do you suppose Angeline will do now?'

'My guess is that she and her boyfriend are already making a dash for the airport. They probably haven't even stopped to pack,' he said drily.

Amy looked at him more shyly. 'And what are *we* going to do?'

His dark eyes suddenly gleamed. 'I can think of several things I'd like to do at this particular moment.'

'No,' she said firmly. 'Not that I don't want to,' she went on, her own gaze very bright now, 'but there really are a lot of things that we need to sort out.'

'How can we sort out something that we don't even understand?'

'*I* understand it,' she said at once. 'I've understood it for a long time now.'

Benedict looked interested. 'Do you want to explain it to me?'

'It's actually very simple,' Amy said, her voice quite calm, although her heart was thumping away inside of her. 'This is love—and it's the real thing. I don't know how it happened or why it crashed down on me so fast, but that's what it is. At least, it is for me. I don't know how you feel about it.'

'I thought I'd made it fairly plain,' Benedict said, one eyebrow delicately drifting upwards again.

'Well—yes,' she said, getting slightly flustered as his dark gaze rested on her face. 'But going to bed isn't the same thing as love, is it? At least, not for men. And probably not for quite a lot of women.'

'No, I suppose not,' he agreed. There was a definite glint of amusement in his gaze now, and that rather annoyed her. This was meant to be a serious conversation! They weren't going to get anywhere if he began laughing at her.

'So what I want to know is——' she began firmly. Then she stopped. This was all going wrong. It was beginning to sound as if she was delivering some kind of ultimatum, and she wasn't.

'What would you like to know?' Benedict prompted softly. 'If my intentions are honourable?'

'No, of course not,' Amy said rather crossly. 'That's silly. I just want to know——' She stopped again. What she wanted to know was if, by some major miracle, *he* felt the same way about *her*. It probably wasn't possible, of course. And she was actually scared to ask the question in case he gave her an answer that she didn't want to hear.

Benedict was openly grinning now, and that really annoyed her. In fact, there were a lot of things about him that annoyed her. Perhaps she was making a big mistake. Maybe it wasn't love, after all, but only some crazy illusion . . .

As if he could sense her sudden uncertainty, Benedict took a couple of steps forward, bent his head, and very thoroughly kissed her. It was several minutes before he finally released her again, and by then Amy was completely sure of one thing. This was love, all right! Nothing else could make her feel the way she did whenever he came anywhere near her. And it wasn't just a physical love, although that was certainly a big part of it, and *very* nice.

Benedict was breathing a little unsteadily by this time. He stepped back from her and looked down at her ruefully.

'Do you think that we need to say anything at all after that? Well, perhaps we do,' he went on, answering his own question. 'At least, I do. The only trouble is, I'm not at all sure what to say! Nothing like this has ever happened to me before. I'm not sure that I even believe that it's happened now. Every time I look at you, though, I have to believe it! I sure as hell don't understand it, and I don't suppose you do, either. But I suppose we'll get used to it as we go along, and perhaps we'll even be able to make some sense of it as the years go by.'

'Years?' gulped Amy.

'I don't think this thing between us is going to go away,' Benedict said gravely. 'It looks as if we're going to have to get used to the idea of a very long-term relationship. And one that's also likely to end up as very legal.'

'Legal?' she squeaked.

'At least it'll please my parents,' he said cheerfully. 'They were beginning to think that I was never going to settle down into respectability.'

'I don't think that you're ever going to be entirely respectable,' Amy replied rather faintly. 'And are you really sure that you want to settle down?'

'I think that, with you, I'm going to want a lot of things that I was never particularly interested in before.'

'And does it have to be *me*?' she asked in a suddenly nervous voice. Then she wished that she hadn't asked that. What if he said no? Or gave some evasive answer that would always leave her wondering?

Benedict's reply was quite unequivocal, though. 'Yes; it has to be you,' he said without any hesitation.

But Amy still couldn't quite believe it, or accept it. 'When we first came to Istanbul, you thought it was Angeline that you wanted,' she reminded him.

'I didn't actually say that,' he replied calmly. 'I told you that I was looking for something—someone—and that Angeline was the closest I'd come to finding it. I suppose it was because she was like you, in some ways. Then I began to look at you—and it suddenly dawned on me that you were the real thing; that the only sensible thing to do was to grab you, and hold on to you.'

'Well, you certainly did that!' she said, with the beginnings of a grin.

'I never meant to,' Benedict said, almost apologetically. 'I intended to take it slowly, but things just suddenly got completely out of hand. And you didn't seem to mind.'

Amy's grin broadened. 'No, I didn't mind.'

'There are a hundred and one things that we need to talk about, of course,' Benedict went on. 'Where we're going to live, how we're going to fit our lives together, what kind of a future we want—and we'll have to meet each other's families. Perhaps I should warn you right now that my mother adores weddings. It's likely to be the main topic of conversation once you set foot inside of their house.'

'I think that I'm going to enjoy talking about weddings with your mother,' Amy said with a contented sigh. Then she gave a small grimace. 'Are you sure that you want to meet *my* family? For all you know, they might all be like Angeline!'

'I'm hoping that they're more like you,' Benedict said wryly. Then his expression changed. 'Would you mind stopping talking for a couple of minutes? I'd like to kiss you again.'

'Are you going to be very polite and ask me every time?' asked Amy, her green eyes dancing.

'This will probably be the very last time,' he growled softly. 'When I'm near you, I'm too impatient to be polite.'

His kiss was unexpectedly fierce, but he broke away from her much sooner than she had expected—or wanted. He saw the look of disappointment on her face, and gave a small grunt of frustration.

'Don't look at me like that. I'm trying very hard to hold on to some kind of self-control, but I think I'm going to need some help.'

'What kind of help?' she asked innocently.

Benedict's eyes darkened. 'About the only thing that's going to work right now is if you leave me on my own for a while. I think you'd better go back to your own room and stay there.'

Without a word, Amy walked over to the door. She didn't open it and leave the room, though. Instead, she turned the key in the lock, and then slid the key down her neck.

'You know what you're doing?' Benedict warned huskily.

'Of course I know,' she said happily.

'I still think that you should give me that key.'

'Find it,' she invited.

And he did, eventually. But by then he had forgotten why he had wanted it. And Amy had forgotten everything except that she loved this man beside her and, incredibly, it seemed that he loved her too.

Dreamily, she decided that Istanbul had certainly lived up to its reputation of being a city of mystery and romance.

POSTCARDS FROM EUROPE

HARLEQUIN PRESENTS®

Travel across Europe in 1994 with Harlequin Presents. Collect a new Postcards from Europe title each month!

Don't miss
YESTERDAY'S AFFAIR
by Sally Wentworth
Harlequin Presents #1668

Available in July wherever Harlequin Presents books are sold.

Hi!

I arrived safely in England and have found Nick. My feelings for him are as strong as ever, but he seems convinced that what we once shared belongs in the past. My heart won't accept that.
                    Love, Olivia

HPPFE7

Fifty red-blooded, white-hot, true-blue hunks
from every State in the Union!

Look for MEN MADE IN AMERICA! Written by some of
our most popular authors, these stories feature fifty of
the strongest, sexiest men, each from a different state in
the union!

Two titles available every other month at your favorite
retail outlet.

In May, look for:

KISS YESTERDAY GOODBYE by Leigh Michaels (Iowa)
A TIME TO KEEP by Curtiss Ann Matlock (Kansas)

In June, look for:

ONE PALE, FAWN GLOVE by Linda Shaw (Kentucky)
BAYOU MIDNIGHT by Emilie Richards (Louisiana)

You won't be able to resist MEN MADE IN AMERICA!

INDULGE A LITTLE 6947 SWEEPSTAKES
NO PURCHASE NECESSARY

HERE'S HOW THE SWEEPSTAKES WORKS:
The Harlequin Reader Service shipments for January, February and March 1994 will contain, respectively, coupons for entry into three prize drawings: a trip for two to San Francisco, an Alaskan cruise for two and a trip for two to Hawaii. To be eligible for any drawing using an Entry Coupon, simply complete and mail according to directions.

There is no obligation to continue as a Reader Service subscriber to enter and be eligible for any prize drawing. You may also enter any drawing by hand printing your name and address on a 3" x 5" card and the destination of the prize you wish that entry to be considered for (i.e., San Francisco trip, Alaskan cruise or Hawaiian trip). Send your 3" x 5" entries to: Indulge a Little 6947 Sweepstakes, c/o Prize Destination you wish that entry to be considered for, P.O. Box 1315, Buffalo, NY 14269-1315, U.S.A. or Indulge a Little 6947 Sweepstakes, P.O. Box 610, Fort Erie, Ontario L2A 5X3, Canada.

To be eligible for the San Francisco trip, entries must be received by 4/30/94; for the Alaskan cruise, 5/31/94; and the Hawaiian trip, 6/30/94. No responsibility is assumed for lost, late or misdirected mail. Sweepstakes open to residents of the U.S. (except Puerto Rico) and Canada, 18 years of age or older. All applicable laws and regulations apply. Sweepstakes void wherever prohibited.

For a copy of the Official Rules, send a self-addressed, stamped envelope (WA residents need not affix return postage) to: Indulge a Little 6947 Rules, P.O. Box 4631, Blair, NE 68009, U.S.A.

INDR93

INDULGE A LITTLE 6947 SWEEPSTAKES
NO PURCHASE NECESSARY

HERE'S HOW THE SWEEPSTAKES WORKS:
The Harlequin Reader Service shipments for January, February and March 1994 will contain, respectively, coupons for entry into three prize drawings: a trip for two to San Francisco, an Alaskan cruise for two and a trip for two to Hawaii. To be eligible for any drawing using an Entry Coupon, simply complete and mail according to directions.

There is no obligation to continue as a Reader Service subscriber to enter and be eligible for any prize drawing. You may also enter any drawing by hand printing your name and address on a 3" x 5" card and the destination of the prize you wish that entry to be considered for (i.e., San Francisco trip, Alaskan cruise or Hawaiian trip). Send your 3" x 5" entries to: Indulge a Little 6947 Sweepstakes, c/o Prize Destination you wish that entry to be considered for, P.O. Box 1315, Buffalo, NY 14269-1315, U.S.A. or Indulge a Little 6947 Sweepstakes, P.O. Box 610, Fort Erie, Ontario L2A 5X3, Canada.

To be eligible for the San Francisco trip, entries must be received by 4/30/94; for the Alaskan cruise, 5/31/94; and the Hawaiian trip, 6/30/94. No responsibility is assumed for lost, late or misdirected mail. Sweepstakes open to residents of the U.S. (except Puerto Rico) and Canada, 18 years of age or older. All applicable laws and regulations apply. Sweepstakes void wherever prohibited.

For a copy of the Official Rules, send a self-addressed, stamped envelope (WA residents need not affix return postage) to: Indulge a Little 6947 Rules, P.O. Box 4631, Blair, NE 68009, U.S.A.

INDR93

INDULGE A LITTLE
SWEEPSTAKES

OFFICIAL ENTRY COUPON

This entry must be received by: MAY 31, 1994
This month's winner will be notified by: JUNE 15, 1994
Trip must be taken between: JULY 31, 1994-JULY 31, 1995

YES, I want to win the Alaskan Cruise vacation for two. I understand that the prize includes round-trip airfare, one-week cruise including private cabin, all meals and pocket money as revealed on the "wallet" scratch-off card.

Name_____

Address _____ Apt. _____

City_____

State/Prov._____ Zip/Postal Code_____

Daytime phone number_____
(Area Code)

Account # _____
Return entries with invoice in envelope provided. Each book in this shipment has two entry coupons—and the more coupons you enter, the better your chances of winning!
© 1993 HARLEQUIN ENTERPRISES LTD.   MONTH2

INDULGE A LITTLE
SWEEPSTAKES

OFFICIAL ENTRY COUPON

This entry must be received by: MAY 31, 1994
This month's winner will be notified by: JUNE 15, 1994
Trip must be taken between: JULY 31, 1994-JULY 31, 1995

YES, I want to win the Alaskan Cruise vacation for two. I understand that the prize includes round-trip airfare, one-week cruise including private cabin, all meals and pocket money as revealed on the "wallet" scratch-off card.

Name_____

Address _____ Apt. _____

City_____

State/Prov._____ Zip/Postal Code_____

Daytime phone number_____
(Area Code)

Account # _____
Return entries with invoice in envelope provided. Each book in this shipment has two entry coupons—and the more coupons you enter, the better your chances of winning!
© 1993 HARLEQUIN ENTERPRISES LTD.   MONTH2